Praise for the
Bianca Dangereuse Hollywood Mysteries

THE WRONG GIRL
Nominated for the 2020 Oklahoma Book Award

"With both wit and her trademark warmth, Casey serves up the story of Bianca, the eighth child of Alafair Tucker, who flees her native Oklahoma for glamorous Hollywood in the 1920s. Clever, resilient, and agile, Bianca makes her way into films, but en route, she meets a broad cast of characters, including a sleazy villain and a group of spirited, quirky women, all deftly drawn. The reader is transported to the 1920s Southwest, both seedy and sparkly, and it's a thoroughly enjoyable ride!"
—Karen Odden, author of *A Lady in the Smoke* and *A Dangerous Duet*

"Casey's portrait of how stars were born and kept their status during Hollywood's silent era will intrigue film buffs."
—*Publishers Weekly*

"Casey plays up the melodrama and delivers a silent-movie feel to the story...shocking and amusing by turns, *The Wrong Girl* starts a new series with great promise."
—*Booklist*, Starred Review

"With this new series launch, Casey ("Alafair Tucker" mysteries) performs a little genre-bending, penning a coming-of-age tale within the context of a 1920s-set cozy mystery that could just as easily been ripped from today's headlines. VERDICT: Old Hollywood, silent film stars, the Jazz Age, and strong female characters all combine to create a solid read for crime fiction fans of all stripes."
—*Library Journal*

Also by Donis Casey

The Bianca Dangereuse Hollywood Mysteries
The Wrong Girl

The Alafair Tucker Mysteries
The Old Buzzard Had It Coming
Hornswoggled
The Drop Edge of Yonder
The Sky Took Him
Crying Blood
The Wrong Hill to Die On
Hell with the Lid Blown Off
All Men Fear Me
The Return of the Raven Mocker
Forty Dead Men

Valentino WILL DIE

A BIANCA DANGEREUSE HOLLYWOOD MYSTERY

DONIS CASEY

Poisoned Pen
PRESS

For D.K., with great love now and forever

Copyright © 2021 by Donis Casey
Cover and internal design © 2021 by Sourcebooks
Cover design by Laura Klynstra
Cover images © Ilina Simeonova/Trevillion Images

Sourcebooks, Poisoned Pen Press, and the colophon
are registered trademarks of Sourcebooks.

Published by Poisoned Pen Press, an imprint of Sourcebooks
P.O. Box 4410, Naperville, Illinois 60567-4410
(630) 961-3900
sourcebooks.com

Library of Congress Cataloging-in-Publication Data

Names: Casey, Donis, author.
Title: Valentino will die / Donis Casey.
Description: Naperville, Illinois : Poisoned Pen Press, [2020] | Series:
   The Bianca Dangereuse Hollywood Mysteries ; episode 2
Identifiers: LCCN 2020017136 | (trade paperback)
Subjects: LCSH: Valentino, Rudolph, 1895-1926--Fiction. | GSAFD: Mystery
   fiction.
Classification: LCC PS3603.A863 V35 2020 | DDC 813/.6--dc23
LC record available at https://lccn.loc.gov/2020017136

Printed and bound in the United States of America.
KP 10 9 8 7 6 5 4 3 2 1

Author's Note

This is a work of fiction based on an actual event—Rudolph Valentino's sudden death in 1926 at the age of thirty-one. The fact that the handsome, romantic screen idol died so young, so tragically, so unexpectedly, gave him a cultic, almost mythic, status that shook popular culture to the core all over the world at the time and persists to this day, nearly a century after his death. Valentino's short life was full of much more intrigue and adventure than I addressed in this novel, which only deals with the last few months of his life. Many of the events I wrote about actually happened, but I did combine characters and events and compress the timeline. A huge amount of information about Valentino's life and death can be found online and in countless books and magazines, but I particularly recommend *Dark Lover: The Life and Death of Rudolph Valentino,* an in-depth biography by Emily Wortis Leider, 2003.

A rose.

He draws its tender petals across her cheek, then raises it to his face and breathes deeply of her essence. He affixes the thorny stem to his chest by tucking it behind the family crest on his scarlet baldric, then brushes a kiss across her wrist before gently taking her hand.

The queen is the most beautiful woman he has ever seen, tall, slender as a reed, but unbending as an iron rod. Her skin is as white and cool as alabaster, but her limpid eyes are full of sorrow, a deep well of sadness that the errant duke longs to fill with love.

In full view of the court, oblivious to the wrathful glare of King Mark, Duke Fyodor takes the queen in his arms and pulls her close. Not a sliver of daylight separates their bodies as he begins to move with pantherlike grace around the floor of the ballroom in a sinuous, sensuous waltz that draws every eye. The music swells, as does the queen's heart, unable to resist the passion stirring in her breast, so long unmoved. His smoldering gaze holds hers, enrapt, until his cheek presses close to hers, and into her ear he whispers…

"*Cara,* if I do not sit down for a moment, I will fall down."

———

The queen raised her jewel-bedecked arm above her head and sent a tinkling wave at the director. "Cut, cut, cut! We could use a break, here, Rex."

Director Rex Ingram leapt out of his chair, and the music came to an ignoble, bleating end. "Not again. Rudy, you look about as passionate as a dead fish. What is wrong with you today? Yesterday when we did the scene in the palace garden, you were on fire. I thought I was going to have to throw a bucket of water on the two of you. Now, shape up! Only two weeks left on this shoot. Time is money!"

Rudolph Valentino and Bianca LaBelle moved apart during Ingram's tirade but kept holding hands, mainly because Rudy wanted to punch the director in the face and Bianca wanted to prevent mayhem.

Rudy overcame his irritation enough to say, "*Scusi,* Rex. Sorry. It has been a long day and I am tired."

"Well, never mind, we got some good footage today, and we can take up where we left off first thing tomorrow. Besides, Marty Levinson from the publicity department wants to see you two before you go home tonight, so head on over to the front office after you get out of those costumes."

If Rudolph Valentino and Bianca LaBelle had not been two of the most famous and well-regarded actors in the world, both would have been tempted to fall to the floor and kick their heels in frustration. Bianca made do with a moan. Ingram was already striding out of the studio and wouldn't have cared about his actors' feelings, anyway.

"Do you want to sit for a minute, Rudy, before we head to the costume warehouse?"

"All right, just for a minute."

The extras were already emptying the elaborate ballroom set that had been constructed on Stage Nine, but the wardrobe mistress and the dancing master, who had been standing behind the cameras, started toward the actors, both with concerned expressions. Bianca waved them off. "We'll be along in a minute, Caroline."

The actors made their way to the side of the set, where an authentic nineteenth-century, Austro-Hungarian brocade-covered bench sat against the fake wall. Rudy flopped down with a sigh, and Bianca carefully seated herself and her substantial bustle beside him.

"I hate Ingram," Rudy said.

This was no news to Bianca. She knew Valentino's likes and dislikes well. "What's wrong, Rudy? Besides the fact that Rex Ingram is an ass? You haven't been yourself since we started this picture."

"Oh, I'm sorry, *cara*. It is my stomach again, acting up worse today. I have not felt so well."

"Rudy, you've been having stomach problems for months now. Did you see Dr. Moore about it, like I told you to do two weeks ago?"

"Yes, of course. Do not scold me. He says nothing new that he can find. Not to worry because I shall irritate my ulcer. To rest. To not eat spicy food. Ha! I cannot rest, and food is my only pleasure since Natacha left me. My new house, Falcon Lair, it is torn to pieces with the renovation, and reporters, fans, they will not leave me alone…"

"Look, why don't you spend tonight at my estate? In fact, you're welcome to stay at Orange Garden for as long as you want, at least until the remodel is done on Falcon Lair. I know just how to take care of a tender stomach. Besides, Fee is off tonight, and I'd be glad of the company."

"Such a generous offer, *cara*. Yes, maybe just for tonight. You have always taken good care of me."

Bianca smiled. Rudolph Valentino may have been known worldwide as the greatest Latin lover to ever grace the silver screen, but in real life, poor Rudy had always had singularly bad luck with his romances. Bianca knew why, too, and had never been shy about telling him all about it. Rudy was drawn to the wrong kind of woman—or wrong for him, at least. He was attracted to strong, independent, artistic women, and fell madly, instantly, into the throes of *amore*. But as the relationships advanced, his stubborn, old-world expectation of what a woman should be like—gentle, compliant, Madonna-like—ended up driving her away.

Bianca had informed him more than once that you can't tell a woman you admire her for being one way and then demand she change into something else. In her experience, too many men fell into that trap. Especially Italian men. Especially this particular Italian man.

Rudy just laughed at her. "You are one to talk," he'd accuse. Bianca LaBelle, a world-renowned beauty, never had relationships at all, at least not one that hadn't been specifically set up by a studio publicist to promote her image as a woman of mystery and dangerous allure.

Bianca and Rudy had been friends for years, but nothing more than friends. They had both come to Hollywood broke and in trouble, and though he was a decade older than she, each by their own lightning-strike of fortune had gone from completely unknown to incredibly famous at about the same time. For Rudy, one sultry tango in *The Four Horsemen of the*

Apocalypse had vaulted him into the stratosphere. For Bianca, one fantastic, swanlike leap from the queen's balcony in *The Three Musketeers* led to a series of wildly popular adventure pictures about the indomitable world traveler, journalist, and sometime spy, Bianca Dangereuse.

Valentino and LaBelle had met at a party. There was always a party involved in Hollywood. That fateful shindig had been at silent screen legend Alma Bolding's house back in 1922. Rudy was newly divorced from actress Jean Acker (or so he thought) and living with set designer and his eventual second ex-wife, Natacha Rambova (née Winifred Shaughnessy), in a tony house down the hill from Alma's Whitley Heights mansion. He and Natacha had owned a lion cub then and walked it on a leash around the neighborhood every evening, which said a lot about their mutual disregard for convention.

Bianca was Alma's protégé at the time, still living with the star while Bianca's own Beverly Hills mansion was being built, just down the road from Mary Pickford's and Douglas Fairbanks's place, Pickfair.

Bianca had liked Rudy right away. They were alike, both headstrong and restless, eager for adventure, and loved dogs and horses. She appreciated the fact that he didn't have a giant ego like many of the men she dealt with in Hollywood. He was sweet and rather naive and told terrible jokes that she didn't get. The two of them had been trying to navigate their newfound fame, and both were still a bit shell-shocked, unsure of who to trust. They were the hottest new faces on the Hollywood scene. The fact that they both had "it," whatever that was, gave them a kind of kinship.

Now, four years later, their stellar fame had not lived up to its shining promise, and Valentino and LaBelle were like old war buddies. No one who had not lived through the same bloody battles they had could understand their bond.

~ Fame, as it turns out, is not all it's cracked up to be ~

After resting on the brocade bench for a few minutes, Valentino declared himself better and walked with Bianca off the stage and across a short alley to the costume and makeup bungalow. The sight of a beautiful, regal, green-eyed woman in a fake diamond tiara and purple sateen Hapsburg-era ball gown, and a striking man with smoldering dark eyes, dressed in tails with a medal-encrusted red baldric across his chest would normally be no occasion for remark here on the Pickford-Fairbanks Studio lot, where actors of every imaginable stripe wandered the grounds. But these two were not ordinary mortals and passersby who caught sight of them stopped to gawk and whisper behind their hands. Bianca and Rudy no longer noticed. They both were accustomed to being admired, or at least to being objects of intense scrutiny.

Wardrobe mistress Caroline White and her minions were waiting for them when they arrived at the warehouse, and the actors had barely cleared the doorway before multiple hands began removing their expensive costumes—sashes, tiaras, medals, and jewels, Bianca's elaborate wig. Bianca and Rudy chatted comfortably as they were stripped down to their underwear. As soon as the costume elves disappeared with armfuls of clothing, they made their way to their individual dressing nooks to don street clothes and remove their makeup with buckets of cold cream.

Before walking all the way from the backlot to the front offices to meet with the studio publicist, Bianca telephoned to warn that they were on the way. They were told to stay put until a guard could arrive to drive them across the acres of studio lot. If they legged it, they were liable to be so delayed by adoring fans, aspiring actors, and other admirers that they might not make it to their appointment at all.

The head of United Artists' publicity department, Marty Levinson, didn't wait for his starstruck assistant to drool over

Rudy before he ushered them into his office, where he proceeded to drool over Bianca.

Bianca withdrew her damp hand none too gently from Levinson's grasp. "What do you want, Marty? It's been a long day and we're both beat."

Levinson pouted a bit but got down to business. "Listen, Miss Pickford thinks that *Grand Obsession* is going to be a blockbuster. But this is a damned expensive shoot..."

"What, expensive?" Bianca interrupted. "If we were shooting in Vienna, like we ought to be, that would be one thing, but on the Santa Monica Boulevard backlot?"

Levinson was not cowed. "Yes, expensive. The cost for the sets and costumes is astronomical. You know how Mary demands quality. Besides, the salaries for the two of you are through the roof."

"As they well should be." Bianca slid a glance at Rudy. He looked every inch the matinee idol, clad in plus-fours and an open-collar white shirt, his black hair slicked back and shiny as a mirror. He had crossed his legs and relaxed into his chair with his elbows on the armrests and his fingers steepled before him, letting her do the talking. She was more than willing to do so. Rudy was too easygoing about this sort of thing. Bianca returned her attention to Levinson. "You know very well our names are going to make the studio a bundle. Now, what did you want to see us about?"

Levinson sat down on the edge of his desk, amused at Bianca's immediate power maneuver. The two veteran actors knew that they were about to be hustled into cooperating with some publicity stunt, and she was reminding him that they were too big to be strong-armed. He was just the publicity guy. It was no skin off his nose.

"Here's the deal, Bianca. Since Rudy and Pola Negri have tragically broken up, and since you are a famous virgin..."

Bianca and Rudy burst into laughter at the same time.

"Why not?" Levinson said. "A romance between you two would sell a million tickets worldwide."

"Why do you think I have broken with Pola?" Rudy said. Pola Negri was a fiery Polish-born screen vamp whom he had been dating off and on for several months.

"Louella Parsons wrote in the *Examiner* that you two broke up in April."

Rudy gripped the chair arms and leaned forward. "Pola and I are still seeing one another. Besides, Natacha and I may never be together again, even if I do still love her. How will it look to her if Bianca and I…"

"Both Pola and Natacha know how things work around here. Just tell them it's a sham. Better yet, have Bianca tell her, whichever one you really want. In the meantime, what a story for the public. Bianca comforting you, soothing your broken heart. Two lonely people finding one another in this cold, cruel world."

Bianca didn't offer an opinion. She had been paired in the industry journals with infinitely less appealing men than Rudolph Valentino. It never meant anything. But in this case, Rudy really was suffering from a broken heart, so as far as she was concerned it was up to him whether or not to go along with this particular illusion.

"You are both too pretty to do a project together and have people believe the sparks don't fly. This way you can control the narrative."

"Oh, bullcrap, Marty," Bianca said. "You know that no one can 'control the narrative' in this town."

"I don't want to do it," Rudy said. "I love Bianca, but not like that."

Levinson shrugged. "Look, the rumors are going to fly whether you play along or not. 'LaBelle and Valentino together at last,' and all that. I'm just offering you the chance to have something to say about it."

"I'd like to think about it," Bianca said, and Rudy nodded his agreement.

Levinson rounded his desk and sat down. "Okay by me. Go home. Talk to your agents and get back with me by Friday. In the meantime, after the movie wraps, I've set up an interview with the two of you with Jimmy Quirk, the editor over at *Photoplay*, so you'd better decide how you're going to play this before then."

It was well after dark when they left the studio in Rudy's specially made Isotta Fraschini town car, but word had gone around that they were shooting on the lot, so a knot of dedicated fans was standing vigil outside the studio gates. Due to the late hour, only about thirty people were blocking the road, so Rudy told his chauffeur, Frank, to pause at the gate while he and Bianca signed autographs and exchanged a few smiles and handshakes through the car windows. Neither of them got out. They had both had their share of alarming encounters with overexcited admirers.

> *~ A night of respite from the glare of the spotlight ~*

Frank drove them from the United Artists lot on the edge of Los Angeles to Beverly Hills, then followed a serpentine road nearly to the top of San Ysidro Canyon and Bianca's ten-acre estate, Orange Garden. They passed through the tall iron gates and made their way down a winding dirt road for nearly a quarter mile before turning onto the palm-lined drive leading to the California Mission–style mansion. Frank pulled up before the massive entryway, where the stars were met at the door by Norah, Bianca's loyal but snippy maid, and by Bianca's weirdly mixed-breed little dog, Jack Dempsey, who looked like he could be part prairie dog and part something else. Maybe a mongoose. Or a wig. Rudy scooped up the overjoyed pup and tucked him under an arm. Valentino was a dog lover, and he and Jack had always gotten along well. Norah took their wraps and their drink orders—a dirty martini for the lady of the house and, on Bianca's orders, ginger tea for Rudy.

Norah brought the drinks to Bianca and Rudy in the sleek

white, gold, and black living room. Bianca had added a large painting over the fireplace since the last time Rudy had visited—a bright portrait of a woman in a red sweater against a backdrop of snow-covered mountains. Rudy was enthralled. "A new painting! How beautiful. *Che bella.*"

Bianca's eyes followed his gaze. "Ah. I've owned it for a while, but I just brought it out again. I like it."

Rudy laughed. "She is lovely. *Robusto*, no?"

Bianca treated him to the briefest flash of her heart-stopping grin. "Robust! She is, isn't she? That was painted by my friend Tamara de Lempicka. I met her last year when I did the movie *Apache Dancer* in Paris. She took me to a wonderful show of decorative arts, the *Exposition Internationale des Arts Decoratifs et Industriels Modernes*. It was the most exciting thing—I went every day that I wasn't shooting and spent a boxcar full of money on art, I'm afraid."

"Ah, Paris. I would love to go back. And such art. I love the new art. I've read of this show. I wish I had seen it."

Bianca's usual cool expression gave way to one of unstudied delight as she remembered. "Oh, it was fantastic, a whole new way of seeing. Everything was so simple and clean and straight-forward. I loved everything about it, the lines, the colors. It made me feel hopeful."

"Hopeful," Rudy repeated, not understanding.

She glanced at him. "There's something desperate about the times, don't you think? All this gaiety, it's not real. Cynical. Desperate." She folded her arms. "Since the war."

Rudy shrugged. "I feel the same. But I thought it was only me."

"Hardly." Bianca sat down on the long white couch and crossed her legs. In her daily life Bianca LaBelle liked to wear trousers and boots, no makeup, a colorful scarf around her cropped sable curls, like she was going on a six-month safari. Somehow wearing trousers made the actress's lithe, long-legged form look even more feminine. She gestured for Rudy to join her. Instead he continued to wander around the room with the happy pooch under his arm, examining the accoutrements.

"All this decor is certainly not like the house I grew up in," Bianca said. "My mother's house...well, she didn't exactly decorate. My mother's house grew like a mushroom. It's quite wonderful, really. Everything in the house has a purpose. Nothing goes to waste. Most of my friends here in California are very wasteful."

He nodded at a side table, at a small bronze statue of a demure naked girl sitting on a rock with her knees drawn up under her chin. "And what is the purpose of this, then?"

He was teasing her, and she knew it. She smiled. "To gladden the eye. What could be more useful than that?"

"And who is this?" He reached past the naked girl and picked up a photograph of a woman with her dark hair swept up into a messy bun and a don't-mess-with-me look in her dark eyes. There was a familiar cast to her features.

"That's my mother," Bianca said.

Rudy couldn't tell by her inflection how Bianca felt about that. "Is she still living?"

"Yes, she is."

"Do you miss her?"

"I do. I miss my whole family. I see them when I can, but it isn't enough."

He sighed. "My mamma is no longer alive, nor my papa. I still weep when I think of my gentle mamma. How I miss her."

"Do you still have family in Italy?"

"My sister, Maria, lives in Milan. My brother, Alberto, and his wife and son are to come to America in a few weeks and stay with me at Falcon Lair for a while. I hope the house is in a fit state by the time they arrive. You have family still in Oklahoma?"

She laughed. "Do I ever. Besides my parents, I have seven sisters and two brothers and more nieces and nephews than you can count. On rare occasions, one or another will come and visit me here in California."

"Do you ever go back?"

"I do, whenever I can sneak in without making a fuss, which is seldom." Her cheeks reddened. "After the way I hurt my parents, I was pretty nervous the first time I went home. A few years ago, now."

"You, hurt someone? I cannot imagine."

"I ran away from home without a word. I was just a stupid kid. I told you about that, didn't I? It nearly killed my mother. A couple of my sisters are still sore at me. But when I finally did try to make amends..." She looked away. "...I thought I'd have to beg forgiveness, but my folks were swell. My mother wouldn't let me out of her sight and stuffed me with food like a foie gras goose. Talk about the prodigal returning. They killed the fatted calf."

"What is a fatted calf, and why did they kill the poor creature?"

Bianca's gaze returned to Rudy's face and she smiled. "What's the matter with you, Rudy? Haven't you ever read a Bible?"

"Of course. I was raised a good Catholic. I know the story of the prodigal son, but we do not have a fatted calf in Italian."

"Oh, I guess not. 'Fatted calf' is just how they said 'a nice piece of veal' in the King James Bible. I was raised a good Protestant. I can't say it took, and I can't say I feel bad about that. But I can quote you chapter and verse with the best of them. I keep in touch with my family, but I seldom go back to Oklahoma anymore. I'd rather pay for them to come visit me. You know how it is. I can't go anywhere without fending off a mob, and I don't like doing that to my parents. They don't like it, either. Besides, it's too painful."

Rudy knew only too well. "I, too, went home to Italy three years ago, with Natacha. I had not been home for ten years. No one knew who I was, so people in the villages we passed through were more interested in my automobile than in me. I was happy to see my sister and brother, but it was a hard trip. It made me sad. Nothing had changed. Everything was the same. Except me." He set the frame back on the table. "You look like your mamma. She is beautiful. *Formidabile.*"

That made Bianca chuckle. "She's formidable indeed."

Rudy picked up another photo, a small, gap-toothed boy with a big grin and a mop of dark curls. "And who is this *bambino*?"

Bianca stood up. "Put down the dog and stop fingering my stuff, Rudy, and let's go into the kitchen and get you something to eat."

The mention of food reminded Rudy of his earlier discomfort, and he put a hand on his flat stomach. "I do not think I can eat."

"I think you'd better. An empty stomach is no good for an ulcer. I'll make something that will soothe that ache, and we can talk about Marty's proposal."

Rudy smiled. If there was anything he enjoyed, it was being fussed over.

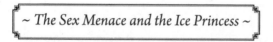

~ *The Sex Menace and the Ice Princess* ~

As Bianca bustled around her state-of-the-art kitchen and Rudy watched from his perch on a stool at the white marble island, they made small talk in French, which Rudy spoke like a native and Bianca was eager to practice. As soon as *Grand Obsession* wrapped, in a mere two weeks, Bianca would begin filming her next Bianca Dangereuse feature. After that, she planned to take a long-delayed vacation. No, she didn't know where she was going yet. Maybe back to Paris. Maybe she would invite her mother to come to California for a few days.

Rudy encouraged her to go to Europe. He had last been to France in '23, and he was longing to return. But he had to go to New York soon for the premiere of the highly anticipated movie he had finished earlier in the summer, *The Son of the Sheik*. Afterward, he thought he would stay in the city for a while to visit friends.

After twenty minutes of chatting about nothing much, Bianca set a bowl of steaming, garlicky cabbage soup in front of him and took a seat next to him.

Rudy was highly skeptical. "I hope you are joking me. This smells like feet."

Bianca snorted a laugh. "Don't be such a snob. Trust me, it will make you feel better."

He made a face and pushed it away. Bianca pushed it back. Rudy threw up his hands. "A glass of milk, *cara*. I drink a glass of milk for soothing my stomach."

"This is much better. You're such a baby! Take a sip. It's really quite tasty."

In truth, Rudy had no objection to either cabbage or garlic. He was something of an Italian cook and self-proclaimed connoisseur himself, and could make a mean *verza stufata*. But he did enjoy giving Bianca a hard time. He dipped out a spoonful of soup and took a tentative sip. A moment to savor. He raised his eyebrows and rocked his head from side to side. Not bad.

Bianca got down to business as Rudy ate. "What do you think of Marty's proposed publicity stunt? Our agents will push us to do it."

"I do not like it," he said, between bites. "Why must we be lovers? Why can we not be what we are? The best of friends."

She propped her chin on a hand. "What, the ice princess spends weeks working with the great romancer of women and they don't immediately fall into each other's arms?"

Rudy didn't look at her as he took a moment to blow on his soup and consider his answer. "You are sarcastic, I think. I am exhausted of being a sex symbol, of being mobbed everywhere I go, of being called either a seducer or an effete 'powder puff.' This great lover image, this sex menace, it embarrasses me."

Bianca only half-believed that. "It's made you very rich and very famous."

"Yes, but also it has made me very tired and cost me dearly. You like this 'ice princess' thing?"

"I do, actually. I'd rather have that image than be thought of as a flapper or a party girl like Louise Brooks. It gives me an excuse to keep people at arm's length if I want to. I admit it is a problem when some boob decides he's the very guy to thaw my glacial heart." She shrugged and admitted, "There are so many of them."

"And that is just what the studio wants me to be for you."

Bianca's hand dropped to the countertop. "All right, then. When we talk to Jimmy Quirk, we'll tell the truth and let the chips fall where they may."

"I am glad you see it my way, *cara*. And this soup, it does help. *Miracolo!*"

"See? I told you." She stood up. "It's a beautiful night, darlin'. Come outside with me and let's sit by the pool for a while before bed."

> ~ *That should have been the first thing you said!* ~

It was a beautiful California summer night indeed, clear and moonlit, still relatively warm after a hot day, though the temperature was dropping quickly. Bianca and Rudy strolled together around the grounds, through the small orange grove that gave the estate its name, and Bianca took the opportunity to show Rudy the vegetable garden near the house that she had planted and tended herself. It was burgeoning right now, and Rudy exclaimed over her beautiful crop of tomatoes and eggplants, vowing to make his famous spaghetti sauce for her if she would promise to give him some of her canned tomatoes. They visited Bianca's small stable and said hello to her four riding horses. Both stars were expert riders and had spent many happy hours riding through the hills together. Bianca suggested a nighttime ride, but Rudy demurred, too weary at the moment.

They wandered back toward the house and sat down next to one another on chaise lounges next to the pool.

Rudy sank back and heaved a mighty sigh. "I am tired, *cara*. I will have to find my bed soon."

"Everything in your usual guest bedroom is ready when you

are, hon. You know the way." Bianca had just reclined, but now she popped back up into a sitting position. "Look at that moon. *Que bella!* As for me, it's such a lovely, warm night that I think I'll take a swim. Come on, Rudy."

"*Sei pazza,*" he said, amused.

"I'm not crazy." She pulled her boots off and stood up. "What could be more relaxing than floating your cares away?" She proceeded to strip off her trousers and shirt and dove into the pool clad only in her camiknickers. The full moon shimmered on the water and glistened off of Bianca's bare shoulders as she began to swim, a strong, smooth crawl across the blue and white mosaic-tiled pool.

Rudy stood up to watch her glide through the water. He sighed, moved by the fragrant night, the glint of moonlight, and the beautiful woman. He took off his shoes and sat on the edge of the pool to dangle his feet in the water. "It's cold!"

Bianca stopped swimming and turned over to float leisurely on her back. The silk camiknickers clung enticingly to her body. "It's refreshing," she corrected.

"If Jimmy Quirk from *Photoplay* saw us now, he would believe in our affair, no matter what we tell him," Rudy said.

Bianca continued to float, her face turned up toward the full moon, her eyes closed. "He already does, no matter what we tell him."

After a long, relaxed moment of silence, Rudy said, "Why do you never love, *cara*?"

The question made Bianca swallow a mouthful of water. "Who said I don't?" she said, treading water after a few seconds of splashing and sputtering.

"Do you?"

"Of course I do, Rodolpho. What a question."

"Is it girls you like, *cara*?"

Bianca was surprised by his question, but not offended. Hollywood was rife with lesbians, and rumor had it that Rudy himself was not strictly heterosexual. She didn't know if the rumor was true. Neither one of them had ever tried to seduce the other. They had never discussed their sexual preferences at all. "Not that it's any of your business," she said, "but no, I've never been particularly attracted to other women. Sometimes I think my life would be easier if I were."

Rudy chuckled. "So you have a lover, yes?"

"Not at the moment, no. You?"

"Not at the moment," he admitted.

"Pola told me not long ago that you two are about to become engaged."

Rudy shrugged. "Pola is wonderful. But she runs too hot for me, always exploding like Vesuvius. I like my peace." He sighed. "I think perhaps I shall break it off soon. I need someone who is…less complicated."

Bianca had first met Pola Negri at Constance Talmadge's house in Santa Monica and thought she was a lot of fun. Her English was hilariously twisted, and she had no inhibitions whatsoever. The blame for Natacha and Rudy's breakup lay with both husband and wife, but Natacha was cruel to Rudy in the end, flaunting her affairs in his face. At first, Bianca thought Pola was a good distraction for Rudy after the divorce. Too much of a distraction, as it turned out. She was free-spirited to the point of anarchy, and jealous to boot, which did nothing for the peace of mind of an expansive, friendly, flirtatious man like Rudy.

They eyed one another across the water, unsure of what to say next. Either of them could have had a dozen lovers of either sex in the blink of an eye.

Bianca LaBelle was one careful young woman. Rudy had learned that early on. Valentino was impulsive, overly romantic, and every move he made was splashed all over the tabloids. Bianca did a good job of keeping any bad habits she might have well-hidden. Rudy suspected Bianca had learned the value of sobriety and self-control from her mentor, actor Mary Pickford, one of

Hollywood's most successful moguls of either sex. It was harder to take advantage of someone who had all her wits about her.

Alma Bolding, a once-popular but now fading star who had given Bianca her first break in the movies, was a well-known user and drunk. Which is why her movie career was on the skids. But for some reason, the high life never quite took with Bianca, even considering the fact that her friend Alma was one of its foremost practitioners.

Rudy had been present the first time Bianca had accompanied Alma on one of her weekends of debauchery at Hearst Castle, back in 1922. Bianca had spent the entire time fending off drunken glitterati of both genders and ended up locking the door to her suite at night. She had gained a reputation as a bluestocking after that. But Hearst's mistress, Marion Davies, liked her, and so did newspaper czar Randolph Hearst himself. Bianca was kind, witty, not particularly judgmental, and up for an adventure, adept at sailing, riding, and lawn tennis, even if she did insist on staying sober and wasn't interested in bed-hopping. Her perceived aloofness had made her a challenge for some of the more determined *roués* around town, so she never accepted an overnight invitation to anyone's estate unless she could bring her large and sexually indeterminate guardian, Fee, with her.

It had been that first weekend at Hearst Castle that Bianca and Rudy had discovered their mutual love of dogs and horses. In spite of Rudy's reputation as a hot lover and Bianca's as a cold virgin, the two matinee idols had quickly become the warmest of friends.

Rudy continued, "Was there ever someone… Is there someone who holds a place in your heart like no other?"

Bianca hesitated. "Not really. Most of the guys I've been mixed up with have turned out to be jerks. Well, except one, long ago. His name was Arturo Carrazel. I was just a child, but…"

"You are still just a child, *cara*," Rudy teased. "But you should find your old love, someone who could love you for who you really are, and not this creation you have become."

Bianca ignored the jibe about her age. "I think of Artie some-times and wonder what became of him, though I'm sure he never thinks of me—the real me—at all. How about you?"

"I don't know. There is a girl I have recently..." He let the thought trail off. "But everyone I have ever loved has left me."

The comment took her aback. She knew Rudy to be sensitive and reckless both in life and in love. He usually suffered greatly for a while and then bounced back handily. This seemed different, darker. "What brought this on?" Bianca said.

"I am a farmer in my soul. Did you know that? I meant to become a farmer when I moved to California. But I cannot do it now, not for a long time. I have too many debts and must keep working to pay them off. I cannot keep playing this same lover over and over, not much longer. Soon I will be too old and bald and ridiculous." He looked up at the moon. His dark, liquid eyes glistened in the lambent light. Were those unshed tears? "I grow to hate my life, Bianca."

What a remarkable revelation. She swam to the pool's edge where he was sitting. "What's wrong, Rudy? Tell me. I've known for weeks that something is eating you up."

Rudy was unfamiliar with the phrase, but he nodded. "Yes, eating me up." He dug into the pocket of his plus-fours and pulled out a much folded, wrinkled piece of paper and held it out to her. He didn't unfold it. It was too dark and he was too nearsighted to read it to her, but he had memorized the contents.

"Valentino will die," he recited.

~ I Know a Guy... ~

Bianca hauled herself out of the water to sit next to him on the pool's edge and snatched the paper from his hand. Stars of Bianca's and Rudy's magnitude received thousands of letters a week, most appreciative, some wildly adoring. But plenty were mean-spirited, crazy, or downright threatening. When it came to fan mail, she thought she had seen it all. But this single stark sentence boldly printed in the center of the page sent a jolt through her. "When did you get this?"

"Two days ago. It is not the first, either. I have been getting these awful notes, these death threats, for many weeks. I do not know where they are coming from."

No, Bianca didn't expect he did. No one who received seven thousand fan letters a week opened his own mail. "Have you shown these to George?" she asked, naming his manager and friend, George Ullman.

"*Cara*, people have been threatening to kill me or ruin me or maim me for years. What can George do? These notes, they all say the same thing, like this. 'Valentino will die'. Sometimes they show up in the stacks of fan letters my secretaries give me to read. Sometimes they appear from nowhere in my dressing room at the studio, at my house, on the windscreen of my auto. No envelope."

"Well, you'd better tell him, hon. He should call the police or have the studio detectives look into it. Maybe someone can lift fingerprints from the paper. I don't like the look of this. No wonder your ulcers are acting up."

"No, no. The police are terrible, and the studio detectives are worse. If I tell anyone else, it will end up in *Movie Weekly*. Can you imagine if Louella Parsons heard of these threats? The speculation, the lies, and gossip? I would be hounded even more than I am."

"But what does he want, whoever is doing this?"

"To scare me, do you not think?"

"But why?"

He looked away. "Who knows?"

Bianca knew evasion when she heard it. "You have a suspicion, don't you?"

"Drop it, *cara*. You do not want to be involved in my troubles."

"Listen, Rudy, if you don't want to tell me, that's fine. But I know a private eye who I trust to keep his mouth shut. His name is Ted Oliver. He's helped me out before. In fact, he's still helping me out. He might be able to discover who's sending these notes and why."

"Thank you, *cara*. I will keep your offer in mind. But now let us not think of such things. Let us think of this moonlit night, the sparkling water, and that luscious silken fabric clinging to your beautiful body."

Bianca snorted. "Save your bull for somebody who buys it, Rudy."

Unoffended, Rudy stood up. "Then I am off to my lonely bed. Good night, *cara mia*."

"*Buona notte*, Rudy. Don't forget what I said about the gumshoe."

Donatella, Queen Berengaria's faithful maidservant, runs on tiptoes into her mistress's bedchamber.

"Majesty," she breathes, "I heard a noise coming from the tower. I thought it was the cat, so I went to retrieve her, but found the door to the jewel room open. There is a man." Her voice cracks. "In a mask…"

The queen stands up from her dressing table and pulls a silken robe over her nightdress. "Pick up the lantern and come with me." She throws the order over her shoulder as she strides from the room. "And bring my rapier."

The queen and her frightened servant creep up the spiral staircase in the tower, all the way to the top chamber—the king's treasure room. The stout oaken door stands ajar. No light comes from within.

"But who would have a key, Majesty?" Donatella whispers. "There are only two—yours and the king's."

"Hush," the queen murmurs, and slowly pushes the door open only far enough to slip into the darkened room. She presses herself against the stone walls and lifts the lantern high enough to cast a dim light in the gloom. Gold, silver, fabulous jewels, a royal fortune glistens in the pale lamplight. The queen is still, listening. Silence. And then a noise. A scrape.

"Who dares violate the king's treasure house? Show yourself!" cries the queen.

A brief movement to her left catches her attention, and she turns toward it. A man, masked and clad in black, steps from the shadowy corner.

"Who are you, varlet, and how did you get past my guards?"

The intruder emits a mocking laugh. "Guards, padlocks, and iron doors are no deterrent to a skilled and determined thief, Majesty."

"Not so skilled. My guards are on their way. You are caught now, villain, and will pay with your life."

In the blink of an eye, the thief's slender blade is in his hand. "Not today, Majesty. Now, if you will kindly step out of the way, I will take my leave and you will never see me again."

Without taking her eyes off the thief, the queen holds out her white hand. "Donatella," she says to the servant cowering in the door behind her, "hand me my rapier and fetch the guard."

"No, Majesty, do not do it!" the girl protests, but the queen stamps her foot, imperious, and the quaking maid lays the hilt of a wicked Swiss rapier in her hand before disappearing at a run down the winding stone staircase.

The queen places a hand upon her hip and points the blade at the intruder. "You will surrender."

"Ha! Give over, your Majesty, and step aside. I would hate to have to stab the most beautiful monarch in Europe."

"You may try." The queen lifts the skirt of her dressing gown to free her movements and lunges forward. The thief parries skillfully before the point of her blade can pierce his heart. She thrusts again and he parries and dances away with an insouciant grin. But the queen is not deterred, and the intruder finds himself fending off a swipe that nearly takes off his ear. Queen Berengaria is not to be trifled with. They spar, the metallic riposte of blade on blade, the clash of steel upon steel, echoing from the stone walls.

Her skill is impressive, perhaps equal to his own, but no match for his desire to live and thieve another day. A clever feint catches her off guard and, with one swift movement, he sweeps her off her feet and to the floor. He throws himself on top of her, pinning her sword hand under his body.

"It is a shame I cannot stay longer and continue this pleasant argument, Majesty, but I hear the guards upon the stairs."

———

Or that is what the script says. But the thief's back is to the camera, making it impossible for the audience to read his lips, so what he actually says is, "How about a big kiss, *cara*? You know you want it."

The queen laughs. "Shut up and get off of me, Rudy, you incorrigible flirt."

> ~ Bianca realizes that something
> has changed since last night ~

The director covered his eyes with both hands, exasperated. "Oh, for God's sake, will you two stop fooling around? Cut, Harry. All right, it's almost midnight, so that's enough for today. Early call tomorrow, everybody. I want you here at six. Bianca and Rudy, we'll go over today's rushes in the morning, and if we need to, we can reshoot that last bit before Ostrienski leaps out the window ahead of the guards."

Rudy helped Bianca to her feet as the prop and lighting crew moved in around them. Bianca's ever-present factotum, the inscrutable Fee, who had been observing the shoot from behind the camera, draped a wrap across Bianca's shoulders.

"Excellent work today, Bianca," Fee offered. "Your fans will enjoy that scene. Daring, fearless, just what people expect of Bianca Dangereuse."

"Except I'm not playing Dangereuse in this pic, Fee."

"Honey, to your fans, you're always Dangereuse, whether you are or not, just as Mr. Valentino is always the Sheik."

"What our friend says is true, Bianca," Rudy said. "We are slaves to the parts that made us famous."

Bianca grimaced at this uncomfortable truth, but Fee pretended not to notice. "Do you want me to help you get out of costume?"

"No, thanks. Norah's waiting for me in the dressing room."

"I'll bring the car around, then. About thirty minutes?"

Rudy watched, bemused, as Fee swept off in a cloud of Shalimar wafting from the flowing yellow caftan. "Where did you find that worthy individual?"

Bianca smiled fondly at Fee's retreating back. "When I first came to Hollywood in 1920, Fee was working for Alma. In '23, after I was making enough money to have my place built, I asked Fee to run the estate for me, and the rest is history. Nobody takes better care of me."

"She is a most competent person."

"I couldn't do without her."

"Or perhaps she is a he?" Rudy posed the question with an impish wink.

Bianca raised an eyebrow. "Perhaps he is. Fee prefers to decide on a daily basis. As is her privilege. Or his privilege."

Rudy held up his hands in surrender. "I shall pry no further."

"Rudy," she said, "why don't you come stay at my house again tonight?"

"Not tonight, *cara*. I need my own bed. I will go to my Whitley Heights house."

Bianca felt a frisson of alarm. "Rudy, are you sure you want to be on your own after that frightening note?"

"I am touched by your concern, but don't worry, *cara*. Tomorrow is our last day of shooting, and I wish to arrive at the studio early. Besides, I will not be alone. Frank will be in the room over the garage, and Frederick and Emily are always in the Hollywood house."

"Your butler and cook are both about ninety years old, Rudy. They may be game, but I doubt if they'd be much use if somebody broke in and tried to harm you."

Rudy laughed and patted her on the cheek. "You fuss too much, *tesora mia*. I feel much better today, and as for the other, I can take care of myself. I will see you bright and early tomorrow. Very, very, bright and early."

"Don't forget that we have to talk about what we want to say to Jim Quirk at the *Photoplay* interview coming up."

"How could I forget?"

The actors went their separate ways, and Fee accompanied Bianca partway to her dressing room. "Do you really feel trapped by Dangereuse?" Fee wondered.

"No, not really. I love playing Bianca Dangereuse. I love living her exciting life, but I would rather people not think that I am her."

"Well, Dangereuse and the Sheik have certainly made you and Mr. Valentino rich and beloved."

"True. And I'm very grateful. Dangereuse saved me from an uncertain future."

"What was the concern about Mr. Valentino being alone tonight?"

"I'll tell you all about it later. Something's very wrong with Rudy, Fee. He's in danger. I can feel it."

But Rudy did not speak of the threatening notes again, and later, when Bianca questioned him about them, he dismissed her out of hand and refused to discuss it. In fact, he seemed very much his usual self, warmhearted, boyish, and flirtatious. "I have made a decision, *cara*," he told her. "A simple life for me from this moment on." Since Rudy no longer seemed concerned, Bianca put her own worries aside and they finished *Grand Obsession* ahead of schedule.

> "I figure that if a girl wants to be a legend,
> she should just go ahead and be one."
> ~ Calamity Jane ~

Two days after their movie wrapped, Rudy and Bianca met with the editor of *Photoplay*, James Quirk, at Bianca's favorite Italian restaurant in Los Angeles, Rusticana. The restaurant had a palm-shaded private patio in the back where they could talk in peace and eat some very nice *pasta e fagioli*. Jimmy Quirk had a good relationship with both Rudy and Bianca. Rudy considered him a good friend, and Bianca, though more skeptical, liked him better than most industry journalists. Quirk was tactful and not given to indulging in baseless gossip, and that went a long way with two people who were continually in the spotlight.

Each of the industry magazines, including *Photoplay*, had its own celebrity journalist and gossip columnist, each with his or her own style and inclination toward sensationalism. But Quirk was not only a managing editor, he was a warm guy who seemed genuinely interested in those who made a living in the motion picture business, and he had developed several close friendships with some Very Big Names.

After the *antipasti* and a leisurely catching up on family and friends, Quirk laid his notebook on the table and jotted down the words *Interview LaBelle Valentino* before directing his first question to whomever wanted to answer. "Tell me about *Grand Obsession*."

Bianca and Rudy spent several minutes devouring minestrone and describing the plot of their movie, such as it was, in enthusiastic detail.

~ The Action! The Adventure! The Romance! ~

"It's a fun shoot," Bianca added. "I always enjoy doing these swashbuckling pictures. Any picture in which I can ride a horse is jake with me. There was a good atmosphere on the set, and it was nice to work with Rudy at last. He's one of the few people who enjoys horses as much as I do."

"Rudy, talk is that *Grand Obsession* is going to be a classic. Do you agree?"

"One can never tell how the audience will receive a picture, but I did enjoy working on *Grand Obsession*. A wonderful spirit was present, as Bianca said. The actors, the crew were all helpful and unselfish. And I am so glad to finally work with my dear friend, Bianca, the kindest of women. Besides, she is a great actress and working with a great actress makes me a better actor."

Bianca listened to Rudy's praise with a rising feeling of gratitude and some surprise. She had worked with many famous actors, most of whom would have been happy to elbow her right out of the scene. She had learned early on that the way to succeed in Hollywood was to be as nice as she could to the crew on set, generous as possible to yeoman actors, and as pushy and overbearing as she could be with the big egos, of whom there were distressingly many.

She could feel by the rising heat in her cheeks that she was blushing. "Rudy is so kind…"

Quirk spoke over her. "Tell me, Bianca, what do you do to keep from letting all the adulation turn your head? Because it seems to me that everyone is in love with you, men and women both."

Bianca cast a glance at Rudy, who gave her a knowing smile. It was the kind of question they were both asked all the time. "No one is in love with me, Jim. They're in love with the picture of me on the screen. If you have any brains at all, you can't believe in your own reputation, because people adore a lot of silly things. You can't take any of it too seriously."

Rudy sighed. "It is true also for me. They do not love me. I am merely the canvas on which women paint their dreams."

Quirk gave Rudy an amused glance before he said, "Tell me, Bianca, is it ever confusing that your most famous character has the same name as you?"

Bianca arched a shapely eyebrow. Such an obvious question, but she could not remember ever being asked about this before. "Sometimes. That's why I usually just call her Dangereuse, to distinguish the character from the actress."

"How did that come about?"

She laughed. "Blame Douglas Fairbanks. He and Mary Pickford wanted to produce a series with an intrepid girl adventurer, and he liked the way I had done a bit scene in *The Three Musketeers*, where I jumped off a balcony. They thought I had the qualities they were looking to give the character—I can ride and leap off things and generally bang myself around—so Doug started calling her Bianca Dangereuse, and it stuck. I don't think the character had a name until after Doug and Mary offered me the part."

"How much of the real you, Bianca LaBelle, is in Bianca Dangereuse?"

"Sometimes I think there's more of the real me in Dangereuse than there is in LaBelle."

"Speaking of defining parts, Rudy, you have said in the past that you were not enthusiastic about reprising the sheik. What changed your mind?"

Bianca struggled to keep from smiling as she waited to hear Rudy's answer. Years earlier he had told her that he'd murder anyone who tried to get him to play the sheik again.

He shrugged. "They offered me a lot of money, and I have many debts." Quirk began to scribble, but Rudy put out a hand to stop him. "No, wait. Say this. I was persuaded by the artistic script by June Mathis and Frances Marion, both of whom I love, and I wanted to work with Vilma Banky."

Quirk did not raise his head as he jotted down the new answer.

Rudy's original sentiment might or might not appear in print. He'd find out when the issue hit the newsstands.

"Rudy, I've heard that you'd like to do more serious pictures."

"Yes, motion pictures could be as great an art form as painting or music or traditional theater. I'd do *Hamlet* in my pajamas if that was the only way they would let me. This Latin lover image is ridiculous." He chuckled. "I don't know anything about women. Any man who says he does is either a liar or an imbecile."

"Bianca, do you feel the same way about men?"

Her green eyes narrowed. Who knows anything about anyone, she thought. She said, "Men are simple creatures, Jim. What's to understand?"

Rudy barked out a laugh. "So true, *cara.*"

"You two have been friends for a long time, but this is the first time you've been in a picture together. You're both single now, and I hear that Rudy is spending more and more time at Orange Garden with you, Bianca. I think all your readers would love to know if there is a romance brewing between the two most desirable people in Hollywood."

She knew it was coming. They had been warned. Bianca may have liked James Quirk better than many of the other Hollywood journalists, but by this time she had had enough and found herself struggling to remain gracious. She was asked something similar about every male co-star. She supposed that by now she should be used to the same questions over and over, ad infinitum.

"Why, Jim, I'm still just a slip of a girl, far too young to be thinking of marriage. Besides, Rudy is like a brother. If and when I finally decide to settle down, there are plenty of fish in the sea. I've already had hundreds of proposals, some of the kind that would make your hat pop right off. I've said no to them all. If I had a dollar for every time I've said no, I'd be rich. Oh, wait! I am rich."

Quirk was scribbling furiously, happily setting down her remarks word for word. He looked up, pleased to have unleashed the unfiltered Bianca. "Bianca, you are considered one of the great beauties of the time. Any beauty tips you'd like to pass on to your legions of female followers?"

Beauty questions never failed to annoy her, and she suspected that Quirk knew it. She was twenty-one years old, had good bones and good health and a lot of money. She couldn't bring herself to take credit for the way she looked. "I'd say be sure you're born to the best-looking parents you can afford. Hydration is important, too. I never looked more hydrated than I did after five hours of shooting a chase scene during a raging thunderstorm."

"Bianca, what do you say to a girl who wants to be just like you?" Quirk had stopped writing and folded his hands on the tabletop.

"I suggest she get her head examined and then I call security."

"What is next for the two of you? I assume you will be doing a publicity tour together for *Grand Obsession*."

He directed the question to Rudy, who had been enjoying himself immensely while Bianca was on the hot seat. He wiped his eyes with his handkerchief before he answered. "Yes, United Artists will release the picture early next year. We are scheduled for a ten-city tour in December. But first my darling Bianca will begin shooting another Dangereuse here in Hollywood, and next month I am off to promote *The Son of the Sheik*"

"What cities will you be going to, Rudy?"

"There will be preview showings of *The Son of the Sheik* here in Los Angeles, then I am going to San Francisco, Chicago, New York, and Atlantic City for more previews before general release in September."

"Bianca, can you give us an idea of what we have to look forward to in your next Bianca Dangereuse adventure? What dastardly plot will Dangereuse foil this time?"

"The next Dangereuse adventure is called *The Clutching Claw*. Dangereuse and her sidekick Butch Revelle go to China on assignment from the American government to uncover a spy. Suffice it to say that one of them is captured by the Claw and the other must come to the rescue."

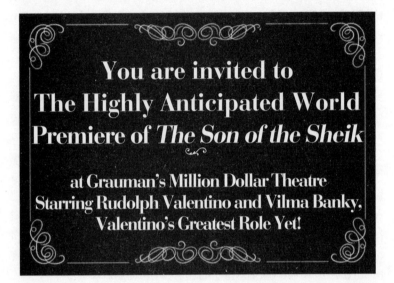

You are invited to
The Highly Anticipated World
Premiere of *The Son of the Sheik*

at Grauman's Million Dollar Theatre
Starring Rudolph Valentino and Vilma Banky,
Valentino's Greatest Role Yet!

After post-production on *Grand Obsession* was done, both stars moved on to their next commitments, which for Rudy meant an advance preview showing of *The Son of the Sheik*, his much-anticipated sequel to *The Sheik*, the movie that had made him a giant star five years earlier. In the sequel, Rudy was playing a double role—an older version of the original Sheik, Ahmed Ben Hassan, as well as his son, Ahmed Junior. Rudy invited Bianca to join his party at the first showing at Grauman's Million Dollar Theatre in downtown Los Angeles. It was a full house, over two thousand people. Bianca didn't bother to bring a date. Pola Negri, all in silver and diamonds, was on Rudy's arm. She kept shooting suspicious looks Bianca's way. Charlie Chaplin brought his eighteen-year-old wife Lita Grey. The irrepressible actress Mae Murray was there, as well as June Mathis, who had worked on the script and had been present during much of the shoot, and of course the film's other star, beautiful Vilma Bánky who played Ahmed Junior's love interest.

Bianca thoroughly enjoyed the picture. In fact, she thought the sequel was better than the original, Rudy's acting much more natural. Young Ahmed loves a Gypsy girl, Yasmine, but when he believes she has betrayed him, he steals her away and has his way with her. He's captured by her father and tortured, swings from a chandelier, bends an iron bar with his bare hands, rides his black stallion breakneck across the Arabian desert (played by the country outside Yuma, Arizona).

Bianca sat next to June, who kept leaning over to whisper asides into Bianca's ear. During one scene in which Rudy leapt onto his rearing horse's back, June murmured, "He loved that beast, but it threw him twice. He's lucky he didn't break his neck."

Mae Murray shushed them, so Bianca didn't respond, but June's comment surprised her. Rudy was an excellent rider. She had seen him keep his seat when his mount decided to try out for the part of a rodeo bronco. He had never mentioned being thrown. She would have to ask him how that happened.

After the screening, the cavernous baroque theatre thundered with applause. Rudy and Vilma stood to take their bows, and Chaplin patted Rudy on the back. "They love you, old man. Say a few words," he urged.

Rudy made his way onstage and made a short speech, nothing much, just thank you so much and I hope you enjoyed it. As he came down the stairs to resume his seat, Bianca's eye was caught by one of the giant decorative vases sitting atop a plinth on the side of the stage. It was teetering, as though someone behind was rocking it back and forth. With a grinding noise, it overbalanced and tipped over as Rudy passed under it. Bianca shot to her feet. "Rudy!"

The cry got Rudy's attention. He braced himself and used a shoulder to deflect the heavy weight from either crushing him or falling into the audience, but it wasn't quite enough. The vase knocked Rudy into the orchestra pit. There was a collective gasp and everyone in the front row rushed forward to lean over the railing. The vase had missed Rudy's head, but he had fallen several feet to the concrete floor and was out cold.

"Call a doctor, call a doctor," someone yelled. Maybe several people yelled. Bianca was barely aware of anything but the sight of Rudolph Valentino splayed out beneath music stands and scores. Rudy's soft, middle-aged, bespectacled manager George Ullman had leaped over the rail like the Sheik himself and was kneeling over his unconscious friend and client. Fortunately, there were a couple of doctors in the house who offered their services, but Rudy came to on his own after a few minutes and staggered back to his seat to the sound of thunderous applause.

Pola, Vilma, George, and Bianca crowded around his seat as the audience filed out.

"Good lord, Rudy, are you all right?" Bianca demanded. "I thought I saw someone behind the curtain. Did you see it? Did you see someone push the vase?"

Rudy sank back in his chair and blinked, confused by the fuss. "The vase was too close to the edge of the pedestal, that is all. I'm fine, *cara*. I've taken many tumbles worse than that."

"What in the hell happened?" George said. "How could the vase fall like that? I'm going to sue the theater. Can you imagine what would have happened if that thing had fallen on your head? Man, that would have been the end of Valentino."

Rudy stood up. "Don't be ridiculous, George. I'm fine. I am better than fine. Let us go out front and greet my public. Then I feel like dancing. Come everyone, let's go to the Cocoanut Grove and celebrate the success of *The Son of the Sheik*. I will treat you all."

Pola was shaken, but relieved that Rudy seemed to be recovered from his close call. "Yes, darling, dancing! This is what we must do."

Rudy did seem to be perfectly all right, but all Bianca could think about was the note that he had shown her a few weeks earlier, by the side of her swimming pool.

Valentino will die.

Should she take it upon herself to tell George? She put a hand on Rudy's arm. "Rudy, do you think..."

His eyes narrowed. "*Cara*, not now." His tone was sharp, and Bianca withdrew her hand. Rudy's expression softened. "Come, now is not the time for worry, Bianca. Come with us. Let us forget all our troubles tonight."

"Yes, Bianca, you must come," Pola said, though Bianca knew she didn't mean it.

"No, you all go on. I'm tired. I start the Dangereuse shoot tomorrow."

Rudy put an arm around her satin-and-pearl-bedecked shoulders. "I am off for San Francisco in the morning to begin my tour, darling, so we probably won't see one another again until the premiere of *Grand Obsession* at the end of the year."

"Do you want me to see you off, hon? I don't have to go into the studio until ten o'clock."

"I am seeing him off, Bianca," Pola hastened to assure her. "Don't worry about Rudy."

Bianca gave Pola a reassuring smile. No reason to be jealous. "All right, I won't. Not with you to take care of him, Pola."

Rudy partied all night, hard and desperate, like a man facing execution. He left Los Angeles the next day on his U.S. promotional tour for *The Son of the Sheik* As for Bianca:

~ **Women Admire Her**
and Men Desire Her ~
Bianca LaBelle

IS **Bianca Dangereuse in**
The Clutching Claw

Bianca Dangereuse, disguised as a young man in a khaki jacket, boots, and trousers, her wild sable curls tucked under a felt fedora, has received word that her cousin and partner in adventure, Butch Revelle, has been captured by the Clutching Claw and is being held captive in an abandoned peasant house in a small village south of Peking.

Bianca creeps along the perimeter of the crumbling stone fence that surrounds the Chinese farmhouse, built of brick around a central courtyard with a south-facing entrance. Bianca is surprised that the Clutching Claw has chosen such a place for his lair, given his love of luxury. The house has three connecting wings, three sides of a rectangle. The fourth side of the rectangle is a long wall and a large gate, creating the interior courtyard. The courtyard is bare of vegetation. No chickens or other animals to raise the alarm.

In the first pale light of dawn, Bianca can make out the shadowy figures of two of the Clutching Claw's minions patrolling the yard, one making a desultory clockwise circle around the house, the other a more sprightly counterclockwise march. Both are carrying a wicked-looking weapon called a *ji*, a long-handled combination spear and ax, slung over their shoulders. Bianca sinks down behind the fence to ponder her next move, eager to avoid being impaled and/or beheaded here at the ends of the earth, or leaving her cousin to a fate worse than death.

Since one guard's circuit is faster than the other's, Bianca has to watch carefully through a hole in the perimeter wall for both men to be out of sight at the same time. She will only have a moment to slip through unseen, and she has no idea if there are other guards inside the house. She settles her fedora firmly on her head and draws her Luger from its holster on her hip, in case she and Butch have to fight their way free.

Bianca Dangereuse manages to slip past the guards and into the farmhouse where Butch is being held. There is no guard stationed inside the gate. The Clutching Claw must feel quite secure in his own territory. Bianca is seized with a momentary pang of pity for the guards outside the wall. They will pay with their lives for letting her slip by them.

She presses herself against the bricks, listening for a clue to Butch's whereabouts. The muffled sound of voices draws her to one of the wings of the farmhouse. A dim light comes through a high window—too high for Bianca to peek through. Her brief reconnoiter turns up a wooden bucket, just the thing to serve as a step stool.

Butch is tied to a chair in the middle of the small bare room. She stifles a gasp. He has been badly beaten. Clutching Claw is standing with his back to her. He is speaking to Butch, though Bianca cannot hear him well enough to understand what he is saying. Not that it matters.

She steps off the bucket and picks it up by the handle, giving it a couple of swings to test its weight. It is a sturdy bucket. Solid oak. It will make quite a dent in the Clutching Claw's skull. She steps to the door, tenses to make her move, and...

———

Bianca was distracted by a large person in black tails, gold cummerbund, and a gold turban, waving at her frantically from behind the director's chair. Fee was standing next to director Nils Fox, looking alarmed. The Chinese guards stopped their pacing, curious, as Bianca handed the break-away bucket to a stagehand. "Fee! What's wrong?"

Fee barged into the scene with Nils close behind. "Sweetheart, I just took a long-distance telephone call from George Ullman in New York. Rudy collapsed last night. He's in the hospital. George is afraid he's not going to make it."

~ *Events take an ominous turn* ~

Bianca's hands flew to her mouth. "Oh, my God, what happened? I read in *Variety* that he was partying at Texas Guinan's place only a couple of days ago. "

Bianca's co-star, Daniel May, his face covered in lurid movie bruises, and the faux-Chinese Clutching Claw, a tall young Hungarian actor fresh from Broadway, Bela Lugosi, had come out of the farmhouse to join the crowd gathering around Fee.

"They're not sure. Rudy wants you to come to New York as soon as you can." Fee shot a glance at Nils, who was hanging on their every word. "I told George that you're shooting, but he says it's now or never. It's important, honey."

Bianca could hardly speak for the lump of fear that had risen in her throat. "Nils..." she managed.

The director shook his head. "I don't know, Bianca. It's four days to New York by train and four days back, and not any faster if you take the combination airplane and train trip. So, even in the best case, you get there and Valentino has recovered and you come straight back, we'd still have to suspend shooting for at least a week, and probably much longer. If it was up to me, I'd say go, but it isn't. I'll have to clear it with Miss Pickford. She's paying for the shoot."

"I've already talked with Miss Pickford," Fee said, before Bianca could protest. "She says to go. I've made reservations for you on the *California Limited* out tonight. Miss Pickford and Mr. Fairbanks are leaving for New York themselves in a couple of days."

Nils threw up his hands. "Well, then, that's that."

"Oh, Fee, you treasure!" Bianca threw her arms around her majordomo's neck, then did the same to a red-faced Nils, who patted her awkwardly on the back.

"Get going," he said. "We'll do as much as we can without you. We still need to shoot Dan's torture scenes with the Clutching Claw. Just get back as soon as you can, and good luck! Give Rudy my best."

Bianca and Fee scurried off set, a curious pair, Fee in turban and cummerbund and Bianca still in her boyish togs. "Now, tell me exactly what George said," Bianca demanded as soon as they were out of earshot of the cast and crew.

"He sounded scared, Bianca. Rudy thinks he's been poisoned, and he wants you to find out who is trying to murder him."

Bianca stopped walking, stunned. "Before he left on his publicity tour, he told me that someone was after him. He showed me a note that said *Valentino will die!* I asked if he had an idea who sent it, but if he did, he wouldn't tell me."

Fee took Bianca's arm and propelled her forward. "Then why now? Why you? What does he think you can do about it?"

"I told him that I know a private eye who could look into it."

"Who?" Now it was Fee's turn to stop walking as the light dawned. "You mean Ted Oliver?"

"He's the only shamus I know."

"What do you expect Oliver to do? Are you going to get him to go to New York with you? Last I heard, he was still working for K. D. Dix."

Bianca resumed their forward motion. "And not happy about it." K. D. Dix was one of the most notorious gangsters in Los Angeles. "No, I'm not asking Oliver to come to New York. Not yet. I need to get there as fast as I can, and besides, I don't know what Rudy has in mind. He asked for me, that's all I know. How quickly does the…"

Fee anticipated her question. "You're leaving tonight on the *California Limited* to Chicago and from there the *Lake Shore Limited* to Grand Central. You'll get to New York on Thursday morning."

"What if he dies before I get there?" It was a rhetorical question, so Fee didn't bother to answer. There wasn't a more practical way to get from Los Angeles to New York.

By this time, they were practically running toward the parking lot, where Fee had parked Bianca's Cadillac. "I've booked us private compartments on the train and a suite at the Ambassador, where Mr. Valentino has been staying. George Ullman's wife, Beatrice, will pick us up at the terminal and take us directly to the hospital."

"What do you mean, 'us'?" Bianca did not miss that little detail.

"I'm coming with you. Somebody has to watch your back."

"I can take care of myself, Fee," Bianca protested, though she wasn't really upset.

"I know you can, honey." Fee opened the front passenger-side door of the car for her and she slid in. "But that doesn't mean you have to. Norah will have our bags packed and waiting for us when we get home. We have just enough time to change and get to the station."

"Well, if you're coming, I want to take Jack Dempsey with me."

Fee got behind the wheel and pressed the starter. "I figured. Norah's packing for him as well."

> *~ On and on they ride the rails,*
> *to the city that never sleeps ~*

The train left Los Angeles early in the evening. Because of her celebrity, Bianca and her party (Fee and the dog) were boarded early and settled in a deluxe cabin, two sleeping compartments connected by a small sitting room. The Los Angeles to Chicago leg of the trip was by far the longer, the train making its endless way through eastern California, across the top of Arizona, to Albuquerque, Denver, Kansas City. Bianca spent the entire three-day trip in her cabin with her dog in her lap, staring out the window at the infinite vistas, the landscape slowly changing from arid desert, to pine-covered mountains, to endless plains, as the *California Limited* made its way across country.

Bianca had made the California–New York trip dozens of times since she had become famous, but every time she boarded the train, she couldn't help but remember the first time she had ridden the *California Limited* with Alma, six years earlier. She had been fifteen years old and had never traveled in such luxury. Alma Bolding was at the pinnacle of her fame, and Bianca (or Blanche, as she was called at the time) was dazzled and amazed by the royal treatment her party received at every turn. People were falling all over themselves to please the luscious Alma. That was when Blanche Tucker decided that the movie star life was for her.

After years of fame and fortune, both the glory and the horror of it all, Bianca LaBelle had mixed feelings.

> *~ Bianca has a long, quiet*
> *time to ponder the past ~*

James Quirk had probed Bianca and Rudy for secrets about their pasts at the end of the *Photoplay* interview, but neither had been inclined to enlighten him. In the end, Quirk had agreed with surprising good nature to let the line of questioning go. But Bianca had days and many miles to think about the conversation she had with Rudy later that evening, after they had left the restaurant. Things were said that seemed prophetic now, and Bianca couldn't get it out of her mind.

It was Quirk who had brought up the topic of other lives without meaning to. "There are a lot of apocryphal stories circulating about both of you, almost like you're creatures of myth. Rudy, I know you were a taxi dancer and tango teacher when you first came to America."

Rudy made a face. "Oh, I don't want to talk about the dancing. I only did that because I had to. I never enjoyed it."

"But you're so good at it."

"I'm good at boxing, too, and sword-fighting."

"How about you, Bianca? You've talked about your first movie with Alma Bolding and Tom Mix in Arizona, but you've never told any interviewer how you got to Arizona in the first place. A couple of years ago, I read the first profile of you in *Movie Weekly* in which Margo Miles suggested you're a French countess who came to America to get away from an importune suitor, but I've never heard you talk about that. You certainly don't sound French. So, what's the real story?"

Bianca pushed her tiramisu around on her plate. "I'll tell you someday, Jimmy, when you don't have that pencil in your hand."

"Is Bianca LaBelle your real name?"

She put her hand on his to stop him from writing. "Of course not."

"Oh, come on, Bianca. Tell you what, I promise to keep it a secret."

"I don't care if you know. But I do want to protect my family's privacy. I like you, but I don't trust you, Jimmy."

Quirk could tell by the set of her jaw that he was not going to get any more out of Bianca. Not today. "Okay, then. Rudy, is Rudolph Valentino your real name?"

Rudy laughed. "Sort of. I have such a long name that I

shortened it. Besides, no one in America can pronounce my family name."

"What is it?"

"Guglielmi." He grinned. "Go ahead, Jimmy. Say that three times fast."

Later that evening, in the back of Rudy's limo after they had left the restaurant and James Quirk behind, out of the blue Rudy said, "LaBelle means 'the beautiful one.'"

"I know. What does Guglielmi mean?"

Rudy made a disparaging noise. "In English it would be Williams, I think. What about Tucker?"

Bianca laughed. Rudy already knew more about her real background than almost anyone. "It means 'one who tucks,' I imagine."

"I think Jimmy was getting on your nerves in the end. That is how you say it, yes?"

"Yes, and yes. You, he asks about the art of cinema. Me, he asks about makeup."

Rudy heaved a sigh and turned to look out the window, thinking. Bianca spent those few minutes regarding his profile, thinking he really was amazingly good to look at.

She was shaken out of her reverie when he said, "Do you believe that we will live again?"

"What? Are you asking if I believe in life after death?"

He gave a particularly Italian gesture of dismissal. "Life after death, no, not as you are thinking of, heaven and hell and all that. I believe that we each live many lives. That this life is not all we have."

"I wish that were true. I would love the opportunity to try again, to do better than I did this time. But I've read Madame Blavatsky's book on Theosophy, too. I don't believe there are a bunch of Masters running the world from Tibet, and I don't believe the dead can talk to us by tapping on tables."

"Oh, I think there is more to being than we know, my darling girl. I do not believe about the séance, either, but are there spirits on the other side who guide us? Perhaps those we love and have lost still help us. There is another world after death that we cannot see, and we may return to this world if we wish. I want to believe it is so." He gave her a surprisingly shy smile. "I do believe it. I have seen evidence."

She knew he wanted to tell her what his evidence was, but the very thought made her want to cry. She didn't want to hear it. She wanted to believe it, too. But she couldn't. "I don't know, Rudy," she said. "I don't know." She leaned back into the leather seat and closed her eyes. Rudy didn't bring it up again.

All the way between Los Angeles and New York, Bianca turned the conversation over in her mind and wished she had let him talk.

Valentino Dead!
...Is a Scurrilous Rumor!

Doctors Say Rudy on the Mend!
~New York Evening Graphic~

At every stop, Fee disembarked long enough to buy a newspaper. Rudy's illness was big news. In Albuquerque, the headline read, *Rudy Brave in the Face of Death*. In Denver, it was *Valentino's Condition Grave*.

By Kansas City, Bianca was relieved to read, *Sheik Rallies*. George Ullman had conveyed some of the waiting reporters' questions to Rudy and delivered his answers to them in writing. "I feel grateful," Rudy told them, "so grateful to my fans, and feel my inability to repay all the kindness extended to me. They have helped me mentally to overcome my sickness." He sounded so normal that some reporter suggested that Rudy's illness and the daily updates on his condition were nothing more than a publicity stunt.

They had a layover in Chicago before changing trains, long enough for Bianca to place a telephone call to the hospital in New York, but the switchboard was jammed and she couldn't get through. She called the Ambassador Hotel and got hold of Beatrice Ullman, who told her that Rudy was still in danger, but seemed to be doing better. Beatrice arranged to meet her at the terminal's Park Avenue exit and drive her and Fee to the hotel.

They left Chicago for the overnight trip to New York, but Bianca couldn't sleep, and neither could her stir-crazy pooch, who was careening off the walls after such a long confinement. Fee faithfully hunted for newspapers at stops throughout the night. In Cleveland the hours-old evening edition declared, *Rudy Doing as Well as Can Be Expected*. In Buffalo there was not a paper to be found, but a ticket agent who was listening to the radio said that at last report nothing had changed. As the sun rose over Albany, the porter brought Bianca a telegram from George Ullman, warning her that reporters were hovering around Grand Central like flies around a puddle of honey, or something smellier, waiting to pounce on any of Rudy's friends or relatives unlucky enough to be spotted arriving in town. As they neared the city, Bianca pulled her deepest cloche hat and darkest glasses from her suitcase and prepared to make a run for it. When the train glided to a stop at the platform, Bianca stuffed a protesting Jack Dempsey into a soft travel bag and handed it to Fee. Jack Dempsey, the ugliest of celebrity dogs, was well known by the press as Bianca LaBelle's constant companion. His presence would give her away in a second.

She stepped off the train behind Fee, and the familiar smell, sound, and feel of Grand Central Terminal smacked her in the face like an open hand.

She had grown used to the paradisiacal weather of southern California, seldom too hot or cold, just one continuous springtime punctuated by the occasional earthquake or rollicking thunderstorm rolling in off the Pacific. But New York reminded her that there are seasons. On other trips, she had stepped out onto Park Avenue or 42nd Street from this very terminal into driving rain, or needles of sleet, or piles of dirty snow in the gutters.

Today it was hot, a particular big-city kind of August heat, thick, humid, and wilting, the kind that makes the air shimmer above the baking sidewalks, compounded by the smell of diesel, iron, humanity, greasy food. She took a deep breath. She could pick out sauerkraut, meat cooking, and…was that Chinese?

"If I were home," she said, "we'd be picking blackberries about now, all dirty and about to faint from the heat, getting our arms scratched up and dodging snakes and spiders in the bushes. Your hands turn purple and so does your face because you stuff so many hot messy berries into your mouth, and Mama yells at you to quit it, now and get to picking."

"Sounds hideous," Fee said.

Bianca shrugged. "I hated it, then. Now I look back upon it with misty nostalgia."

Fee was busily supervising the unloading of their luggage while keeping an eye on the crowds surging up and down the platform. "I'd rather get my blackberries in an uptown restaurant, already folded into whipped cream."

Bianca laughed. "So would I."

Two porters had loaded all their bags onto a cart and started moving toward the ramps that led from the train level to the street level. "Come on," Fee urged. "The longer we stand here, the more likely it is that somebody will recognize you. In fact, look over there. No, don't! I think that's the guy from *New York Today*. Let's get out of here before he spots you."

No matter how many times she came to New York, the city's incredible energy was always a shock to Bianca, and it usually took her two or three days to acclimatize herself. She had been seventeen years old the first time Alma brought her. It had been like stepping off the train onto another planet. They had taken a taxi to the Plaza Hotel on Central Park South, and after fawning over Alma for a few minutes, the chatty driver had regaled them with tales of the other famous people he had chauffeured over the course of his career. Alma had been raised in the Bronx, so there was a long discussion about how things had changed since she lived here. Bianca had been too awed by the scenery to say much, until the driver asked her, "Where are you from, sweetheart?"

She had looked at Alma, who nodded. *You may speak to this strange creature.* "We came here from Los Angeles," Bianca said.

"That's a famous place. How many people live in Los Angeles?"

"Oh, it's a big town," Bianca said. "I heard that almost a half a million people live there now."

The cabbie pointed to the MetLife Building as they sailed past it. "See that building, honey? There're a half a million people in that building."

Bianca's eyes would have popped out of her head, but Alma laughed, which gave her pause. "You're kidding me."

"Oh, yeah? Well, I don't think you're from Los Angeles, girlie. You sound like a sweet corn-fed baby to me. How many people live in your hometown?"

"Last I heard, there were about eighteen hundred."

The cabbie had snorted. "See those people about to cross the street?"

The memory always made her smile. New York was fun. New York was funny. New York was electric.

Fee directed the Red Caps to haul their luggage up the ramp to the main concourse. It was only seven blocks to the Ambassador from the station, and Bianca would have preferred to walk rather than drive. Traffic in midtown was so congested that walking would have been faster, anyway, but with all their luggage, it was impractical. They were supposed to meet Beatrice Ullman at the Park Avenue entrance to the terminal, but when they reached the concourse, she wasn't standing at the agreed-upon half-hidden spot by a column. Bianca stationed herself with the dog and the luggage pile behind a potted plant. Fee went outside to search for their missing ride and found her double-parked halfway down the block.

"How long have you had to wait?" Bianca asked as they clambered into the rented Ford.

"I've circled the block a few times," Beatrice admitted. "But I finally decided to take my chances and double-park."

"You're lucky somebody didn't cuss you out."

"Oh, they did." Mrs. Ullman was an adaptable creature and had assumed a New York attitude. She shifted into first and pulled out into traffic amidst a cacophony of horns. "Rudy is doing a little better today," she added before they could ask. "He's very anxious to see you, Bianca, but I thought you'd like to check in to the hotel and clean up first."

"I'd rather go straight to the hospital. Fee, Beatrice can drop you off at the Ambassador with the luggage, and you can get us situated while I check on Rudy."

The drive from Grand Central to the Polyclinic Hospital on West 50th was hair-raising, though Beatrice did a good job of dodging swerving cars and buses and trucks and the occasional horse, while not running over one of the innumerable pedestrians who meandered across the busy streets in blissful disarray.

~ *The specter of evil hovers over the scene* ~

George Ullman met Bianca in the hall outside of Rudy's room on the eighth floor of Manhattan's Polyclinic Hospital on 50th and 8th Avenue. The manager looked hideous, rumpled, pale, and unshaven. Bianca's heart sank. "Oh, my God."

George hastened to reassure her. "No, no, he's not dead. He's not out of danger, but he's better, actually. He slept well, and this morning he's been fussing to go back to the Ambassador. The doctor operated on him a couple of days ago. He handled it pretty well, but the doctor told me that his condition had gotten very bad. They're not going to even let him sit up for several days. We've put out the word that his doctors aren't allowing anyone but me to see him, but it's Rudy who asked for no other visitors. He doesn't want anyone to see him like this. He's desperate to talk to you, though."

"Tell me what happened, George."

George removed his spectacles and rubbed his eyes. "It was so fast. We went to see *Scandals* at the Apollo on Saturday, then to a party at Barclay Warburton's on Park Avenue. Maybe one, two o'clock in the morning, Rudy fell ill. Beatrice and I had already left the party. Rudy refused to go the hospital. He made them take him back to the Ambassador. His valet, Frank, wanted him to go the hospital right then and there, but you know how he is about hospitals. Frank called me late the next morning and said Rudy was doubled over in pain and spitting up blood. I called a doctor I know who came to the hotel, but nothing he did helped. Rudy kept getting worse. I called an ambulance at about four thirty in the afternoon and they rushed him here. I've never seen him so sick. The doc thought his appendix had burst, and they wanted to operate right away. It took forever to convince Rudy to let them do it. He was terrified of being cut. Jesus! Turns out that he had a perforated ulcer. If he had only listened to me! Now they think his insides are inflamed. Maybe an infection."

"Oh, Lord," Bianca said. An infection was bad news. While 1926 may have been modern times, the best medicine of the day still had no surefire way to treat an infection.

"He's heartsick, Bianca. He's run himself ragged on this tour. He drinks and smokes too much and hangs around speakeasies at all hours. He's felt rotten on this whole trip, yet he arranged a boxing match here in New York to prove his manhood after the asshole columnist at the *Chicago Trib* called him a pink powder puff. After the operation, I cabled Natacha in France, but she won't come. She's sent him a bunch of nice telegrams, though. Pola calls the hospital ten times a day. She's on a shoot in Hollywood and the studio won't let her leave." He emitted a sarcastic snort. "Or so she says."

"George, on the telephone, you told Fee..."

George interrupted. "I know what I told Fee." He cast a glance at the guards stationed at the door and drew Bianca further down the hall, where they could not be overheard. "Rudy's thought for weeks that someone is trying to kill him. Put ground glass in his food or something. You know what his life is like, especially when he's on tour. He's always surrounded by strangers. He's tried to be careful, but he has to eat. He has to drink. He has to sign autographs and shake hands with people."

"Did he show you the threatening notes he's been getting?"

"Not until just before I telephoned you. I thought he was being paranoid until he let me read one. He said he showed them to you a few weeks ago, before you wrapped *Grand Obsession*, and that you know a private detective who could look into it."

"I do know an op back in California. But this is New York. Do you think whoever did this could have followed him here from California?"

"He thinks so."

"Do you believe it?"

"That someone is trying to kill him?" His nose reddened and for a moment, he couldn't speak. "That someone *has* killed him?" he said finally. "Maybe. He keeps having accidents, strange ones, like that vase falling on him in Los Angeles. His horse would suddenly bolt for no apparent reason, things like that."

George's reaction frightened her, and her stomach lurched. "Has the doctor tested him for poison?"

"After the operation the doc took some stomach tissue for testing. But this stomach trouble of his has been going on for a long time, Bianca, months, even. He'd get so ill, then get better for a while. It's no wonder he's been having these ulcer flare-ups, though. He's been driving himself like a lunatic, like he can't stop for a moment to think. He's so miserable. It's like he doesn't care whether he lives or dies."

"What happened this time that's different, George? If he's been sick off and on for months, why is he suddenly so much worse?"

"I don't know for sure."

"Can I see him?"

"Yes, he's anxious to talk to you."

Rudy was ensconced in Suite Q, the most expensive suite in the hospital, two large rooms and a private bath, a huge mahogany bed and dresser, two easy chairs, plush rugs on the floor. She was shocked at Rudy's appearance. He was gaunt, white as a ghost. His face was dotted with strange red marks. The room was miserably hot. The lone nurse at his bedside was sponging the sweat off his forehead.

He managed a smile when he caught sight of her. "*Cara,*" he rasped. "At last."

Bianca swallowed the lump in her throat. "Would you leave us for a few minutes, Nurse? I'd like to talk to Mr. Valentino alone."

In a fraction of a second, a range of emotions flashed across the young woman's face, from *Who do you think you are, Lady?* to *Oh, my God, it's Bianca LaBelle.* She knew her duty, however. "I'm sorry, the doctor says Mr. Valentino is not to be left alone."

"It's all right, Amy," Rudy croaked. "Miss LaBelle and I have something important to discuss."

Amy looked distressed. "But..."

"I'll just take a minute, Amy," Bianca assured her. "You can stand right outside the open door."

"Well, all right, but just a minute."

Bianca sat down in Amy's vacated chair beside the bed and leaned close. Amy had indeed posted herself immediately outside the door. Bianca didn't care that the nurse would be able to watch her exchange with Rudy, as long as she couldn't hear what they said to one another.

Bianca bent over the bed, her ear close to Rudy's mouth,

listening closely as he whispered, "I've been poisoned, Bianca. Did George tell you?"

"Now, hon, you don't know that for sure. We have to wait for the test results to come back."

"Oh, I do know for sure, *cara*. I've known for a while that someone means to kill me. You saw the notes, and they are not the only reason I know. So many enemies, though, I do not know who. You must help me find out who did this."

"Like I told George, I'm no investigator, but I'll do anything I can to help you, Rudy. But you have to help me. Give me someplace to start, hon."

"Where to start? Who knows? I owe so much money to so many people. So many angry husbands say their wives love me more than them. So many people hate me for such silly reasons. Even Mussolini hates me. Did you know that I have applied for American citizenship? *Il Duce* says I am a traitor to the *patria* and he will teach me a lesson. The notes, you said perhaps I had an idea who sent them. Four years ago, I get a note that says 'pay us seven thousand dollars or we will burn down your house.' This happens all the time in Italy, ignorant thugs. They call themselves the Black Hand. I told them to go to hell. No more blackmail notes, but now I get the death threats. But maybe you must start at the end. The night I collapsed I went to an after-party at Barclay Warburton's apartment. I enjoyed the party, but I felt so bad afterwards. There were many people there I do not know. Talk to Barclay, ask about who he invites. Do you know him?"

"I know of him. He's heir to the Warburton fortune." An ironic smirk appeared. "A cake-eater. A flaming youth. One of the idle rich."

"Now, Bianca, don't be a snob. And don't make me laugh. It hurts. Barclay, I have known him for years, since I come to America. I asked him to come here to the hospital, but he says to George that he is not well either. Besides, I am so tired. I forget sometimes what I am saying even as I say it. Please, *cara*…"

"Of course, hon. I'll do whatever you want. I'll ask him about his guests, if there was anyone there he didn't know, or anything he can tell me that might explain what happened to you."

"Thank you. And maybe this man you know in California, he can help, yes? Maybe find out who has been sending threats for so long?"

"Maybe."

He took her hand. His grip was weak. "Bianca, all these years you have been a true friend. You scold me, yes, but never have you asked anything of me and always you take my side. I tell you, *cara*, find your old love, the one who will love you for yourself. Now I'm tired. I think I shall not go on. But no matter what happens, remember I am your friend and I love you."

She lifted his hand to her lips and kissed it, unable to speak. When she finally stood and left the room, unshed tears left her green eyes sparkling like emeralds.

"What does he want you to do?" George demanded.

"He wants me to talk to Barclay Warburton about the guests at the party he went to that night."

George sat down heavily on a bench against the wall of the corridor. "Yes, that's not a bad idea. There were quite a number of odd people there. Barclay had hired this magician…" His voice trailed off. It was several seconds before he resumed. "…who stuck Rudy with a needle as one of his tricks. Stuck it completely through his arm. It wasn't supposed to hurt." He stood up, his gaze wandering off into the middle distance as he mentally reviewed the events of the past several days. After a long pause, he looked up at Bianca. "Ask Jean about it."

Bianca blinked. "Jean who?"

"Jean Acker. They've been hitting the clubs together since he got to New York. She was with him at Barclay's party. Beatrice and I left before the magician's act, but Jean saw the whole thing."

~ *The most unlikely people* ~

Bianca left the hospital through the loading dock at the back entrance to avoid the horde of reporters gathered on West 50th, waiting for any scrap of news about Valentino's condition, or for the opportunity to pounce on any famous visitor to the Sheik's sickroom. She wasn't so lucky at her hotel. The doorman helped her run the gauntlet from the curb to the hotel entrance through the press of reporters.

A bellhop escorted her to her suite on the twelfth floor, where she nearly collapsed into Fee's arms as she stepped through the door.

She gave Fee an update on Rudy's condition. "He's sure someone is trying to kill him, Fee. He wants me to find out who. He thinks I can help because I said I know a private investigator. Bianca Dangereuse isn't real, you know. And Bianca LaBelle is an actress, not a shamus."

"I'm not surprised he picked you to figure it out." Fee was standing at the drinks cart, mixing a martini, and did not turn around.

"You're not?"

Fee thrust the drink into her hand. "You're a smart girl, Bianca. You know people. You know Rudy's world. You can get access to places others can't. People trust you."

"Yes, but…"

"Slug that down, darling. I'll draw you a nice bath. You look like you're about to fall asleep on your feet. You can think about all this later, when you're refreshed."

She sipped the icy martini gratefully. "Okay, you're right." She took another sip as Fee started toward the bathroom. "Fee, while I'm in the bath, please telephone Jean Acker and ask her to come see me."

Fee smiled. "You bet, honey."

There is something about warm water that takes one out of the present and into some timeless higher plane. Bianca soaked in the long claw-foot tub, luxuriating in the scent of the perfumed bath oils that Fee had added to the water. She leaned back and let the steam float her away and her mind wander on the aromatic clouds, thoughts and memories arising from the depths as they would.

How could such a lovely person as Rudy have an enemy who hated him enough to try to kill him, and in such a backhanded, convoluted manner? Why not just shoot him? Why try so hard to make it look like an accident or a natural death?

What have you done, Rudy, and who did you do it to?

Why do you think I can help? You can hire a private investigator as easily as I can. Is it because I said I trust Oliver, and you don't know who to trust?

Bianca sat up. The most unlikely people are the best at sniffing out secrets. Her father had said that about her mother, who poked her nose into other people's problems, whether it was her place to do it or not. People told her mother things they would never tell the police, precisely because she was unthreatening. Or so it seemed.

"People trust you," Fee had said. Maybe her own contacts in the motion picture world, combined with Oliver's knowledge of the underworld, would work together to root out the truth.

Bianca emerged from her bathroom, dressed in her usual trousers and white shirt, drying her cloud of dark curls with a towel, just as the telephone in the parlor rang, and Fee answered.

"Jean Acker is here," Fee said, replacing the receiver in the cradle. "I told the clerk to send her up."

"That was quick."

Actress Jean Acker was Rudy's first wife. He had met her at a party (of course), and in a romantic haze, had married her in a quickie wedding two months later, long before either was a "name." Unfortunately for Rudy, Jean was a lesbian and discovered on her wedding night that she really didn't want to be anything else. After the ceremony, a lovely celebratory dinner, and dancing until dawn, she locked Rudy out of their hotel room and sobbed uncontrollably while he pounded on the door in a fury. They were married—in name only—for three years, but never lived together as husband and wife for a single day.

Jean may not have wanted to be Mrs. Rudolph Valentino, but she didn't want anyone else to be, either. A few months before their long-delayed divorce was finalized, she had Rudy arrested for bigamy after he married Natacha Rambova in Mexico. There was a splashy trial. It was a Whole Big Thing.

But that was years ago. Natacha was history, and Rudy and Jean had decided to let bygones be bygones. That was like Rudy. He hated strife. He and Jean had been burning up the social scene together, platonically, of course, since he got to New York.

Jean was a small, neat woman with a sleek reddish bob, a second-tier actress who had never broken into the ranks of stardom. But she was colorful and amusing, and in spite of her antics, Bianca rather liked her.

Bianca padded in her bare feet to answer the knock on the door.

Jean threw her arms around Bianca's neck. "Oh, Bianca, why won't they let me in to see him?" she wailed.

Bianca guided her to the couch and gave Fee a discreet signal to bring on the alcohol. She sat down next to Jean and handed her a hankie.

"It's doctor's orders, Jean. They're not letting anyone in right now. He needs to heal after the operation."

"Well, they let you in." Jean stated matter-of-factly.

News travels fast, Bianca thought, then shrugged. What made her think she could do anything on the sly these days? She might as well come clean. "He asked for me. He wants me to do something for him. And believe me, the doctors weren't happy about it. They only let me see him for a few minutes."

"How'd he look?"

"Pretty bad, truth be told. But he was able to talk to me, and he said he feels better. His doctor thinks that this crisis may have been set off by something that happened the night before he got sick, maybe something he ate or drank. I said I'd ask around, maybe talk to as many people as I can who were with him on the fourteenth. The doctor feels that if he knew exactly what happened, he might be able to come up with a more effective treatment." Bianca's eyes widened as she spoke, impressed at herself for coming up with such a plausible story on the fly. No use to say anything to Jean about the possibility of poison. Nobody wanted that getting around. "George Ullman told me that you've gone honky-tonking with Rudy several times since he's been in New York, including that night."

"I have and I did. We all went to the 300 Club after the premiere of Rudy's movie at the Strand. Then the next night we went to a play and then to the party at Barclay Warburton's apartment. That's the last time I saw Rudy."

"I heard about that party."

"It was quite the evening. George Ullman and his wife were there, and Jimmy Quirk…"

"Jimmy Quirk from *Photoplay*? I didn't know he was in town."

"Oh, yeah, he's been following the whole *Son of the Sheik* dog and pony show ever since Rudy left California."

"Did anything interesting happen at the party? How was Rudy acting?"

Jean shook her head. "Everything was fine. It seemed fine, anyway. He was drinking too much, I remember that. And smoking. He must have smoked fifty of his special Turkish cigarettes that night. I could barely see him through the haze. Barclay had hired that magician who's all the rage around town, this fakir from Egypt…the guy said he's a fakir. Maybe he's a fake. A fake fakir. Anyway, the fakir asked for a volunteer to help him with a trick and some jamoke in the crowd volunteered Rudy. He didn't want to do it, but you know Rudy. He never could back down from a challenge. The magician said he had the power to stick

Rudy with a needle and he wouldn't feel a thing. He brought out this hatpin—I swear to God it was eight inches long—and stuck it all the way through Rudy's arm. Rudy yelled, 'ouch,' but he didn't even bleed. I thought I was going to faint. Oh, geeze, do you think there was something on that needle, poison or germs or something?"

"I don't know, Jean. When did that happen? How long was it after Rudy got stuck that he collapsed?"

"I'm not sure. I went home from Barclay's place, and Rudy went back to the Ambassador. But it was several hours at least. If he was injected with a poison, wouldn't it make him sick quicker than that?"

"Good question, but I'm no poison expert. What was the name of this magician?"

"He called himself the Great Rahman Bey. Real weird-looking guy, strange eyes, two different colors. He says he's from Egypt, though he's probably Joe Blow from Schenectady. Barclay'd know. He's the one who hired him to entertain at the party."

They paused to take the drinks that Fee had brought to them on a silver salver. Bianca took a healthy swig of her second dirty martini of the night and closed her eyes. Nectar of the gods. She sat the glass back down on the tray. I'm drinking too much these days, she thought. I don't want to end up like Alma.

"Are you going to tell the doctor about the needle?" Jean said.

"Oh, yeah. I doubt if it was poisoned, but it certainly could have been contaminated somehow. Thanks, hon, that may be a crucial bit of information for the doctors."

"Do you think so? I hope so. Do you think Rudy will be all right? Please tell me the truth. Is Rudy going to live?"

"I don't know, Jean. George tells me he's much improved in the past day or two."

Jean gripped Bianca's arm. "Can you get me in to see him? I promise I won't stay long."

"I can try." Bianca gave her hand a comforting pat.

Jean sank back into the couch after draining her cocktail in a gulp. "I can't say I still love Rudy, but I admire him so much. Who else would be willing to forgive the hell I put him through and still be my friend? I don't know why I did it, had him arrested. He was a big star by then and I wasn't. Maybe I was jealous. I just wanted to make trouble, I guess."

"And draw attention to yourself." Bianca did not mean the comment in an accusing way. If she judged everyone in the movie business who did things just for the publicity, there wouldn't be anyone left unjudged. She'd be a hypocrite, to boot.

Jean gave a self-deprecating grin. "That too. It did gain me some notoriety."

~ The playboy tells his tale ~

Barclay Warburton Jr. lived in a tony apartment building on 80th and Park Avenue, where he spent his days idling about and his nights annoying his high-class neighbors with his rowdy parties. It took Fee a few minutes to convince Barclay's butler that, no, this telephone call was no joke. The actress Bianca LaBelle was in town and wanted to meet with Barclay as soon as possible. Bianca's fame won the day, as it usually did, and after consulting with his boss, the butler told Fee that Miss LaBelle was welcome to call on Mr. Warburton at his residence at her earliest convenience.

Fee didn't like the thought of Bianca visiting a well-known carouser and womanizer alone and on his own ground, but the butler had assured Fee that Mr. Warburton was under the weather and preferred to entertain at home, if Miss LaBelle didn't mind. Fee volunteered to accompany Bianca to the meeting. Bianca declined the offer of a bodyguard and went alone.

She was sorry about that decision when the taxi pulled up in front of Barclay's building. It was widely known by the press that Rudy had been taken ill after Barclay's party, and several members of the fourth estate were slouching against the brick wall beside the canopied entrance. Bianca took a giant breath and plunged into the depths. The doorman, who had been instructed to be on the lookout for her, burst out from behind the glass door to run interference. One guy managed to get Bianca's photograph, and somebody else knocked her hat askew. Otherwise, she made it into the building relatively unscathed. A solicitous assistant manager, outraged on her behalf, escorted her through the lobby and rode with her in the elevator up to the eleventh floor, where Warburton's spacious digs took up the entire east end.

Barclay Warburton shuffled into the parlor, where the butler had seated his illustrious guest. He was dressed in his pajamas and a silk bathrobe, looking anything but rowdy. Bianca eyed the *bon vivant* critically and decided that Barclay was an attractive man, tall and fair-haired, and surprisingly young, closer to Bianca's age than to Rudy's.

Barclay's eyes widened when he first got a look at the actress. He had seen many of her movies and knew she was beautiful, but he was not quite prepared for the sight of Bianca LaBelle in the flesh. Her eyes were a stunning shade of green, made all the more interesting by the flecks of gold glinting in her irises. Her bone structure, high cheekbones, and almond eyes suggested that her forebears sprang from some exotic clime. He was aware of the story that she was a French aristocrat on the lam, but that tale had not been repeated for some years. Besides, her curly, dark hair and olive complexion hinted more of Gypsy than of princess.

Barclay greeted Bianca with great propriety before flopping himself into an armchair across from her. "Sorry, Miss LaBelle, I haven't been feeling well. I have not been receiving visitors, but you said this has something to do with Rudy's illness, that I might be of help? I've been meaning to get to the hospital to see him, but I just haven't been up to it."

Barclay may have been ill, but Bianca noted that he still watched with appreciative pleasure as she removed her cotton gloves, one elegant finger at a time. She took her time crossing her long silk-clad gams and eased back into the cushions. No harm in softening up the respondent. "Please call me Bianca. Yes, Rudy suggested that I talk to you about the party you gave the night he collapsed." She repeated the story she had told Jean Acker about the doctors wanting to know if anything unusual had occurred that could help them tailor Rudy's treatments.

Barclay slouched back with his arms stretched along the arms of the chair and listened with interest. His eyes were swollen, and he did look wan, Bianca thought. When she finished her tale, Barclay sighed.

"I know what they're saying in the papers, Bianca, that the evening before he took ill, I threw a wild party with liquor and showgirls. But it was just a little gathering here at the apartment, maybe a dozen people. We had dual reasons to celebrate. Rudy's movie was a hit, and my divorce became final that very day." He gave a rueful smile. "Rudy, the Ullmans, Jean Acker, and I had dinner at the Colony and then went to see *Scandals*. After dinner, Rudy said he felt rotten and nearly went back to the hotel, but I had already asked a few friends over. James Quirk, Marion Banda, a couple of others I'm sure you've never heard of. I had hired a famous magician, Rahman Bey, to entertain at the party." Barclay leaned forward, took a playbill off the coffee table, and handed it to Bianca. It was a souvenir program touting the fakir's appearance at New York's Selwyn Theatre in May. "He's an Egyptian who's been performing around the city all summer to sensational reviews. Rudy didn't want to miss the show. He perked up as the evening went on, acted like he enjoyed himself. Certainly bent his elbow quite a bit, y'know. He was complaining of not feeling well, but he didn't seem all that sick when he left to go back to the Ambassador. The Ullmans left early, and Jean went her own way after everyone else left. I didn't learn that Rudy had collapsed until his valet telephoned me on Sunday morning."

"Where'd you get hold of this Rahman Bey magician?"

One blond eyebrow cocked. "My pal Richie Wilcox saw him perform at the Selwyn back in June. He told me that the show was simply boffo. The fakir takes long needles and sticks dozens of them through his own cheeks until he bristles like a porcupine. Last month he had himself sealed up in a metal box and dropped into the Dalton Swimming Pool for an hour. I thought it'd be fun to have him entertain at the party, so I had my secretary make the arrangements."

"What did you think of him?"

"He was keen. He looked the part of a fakir, for sure. Long hair, beard. Odd eyes. One was dark brown and the other kind of yellow."

"Jean and George both told me that he stuck Rudy with a needle."

"Indeed, he did. The old fella asked for a volunteer and some wag in the back hollered out Rudy's name. I don't think Rudy wanted to do it, but after that columnist in Chicago cast dispersions on his manhood, he probably felt like he had to show how brave he was. I felt sorry for him. Must be hard to have everybody looking at you all the time, eh?" He hesitated. "Look who I'm telling."

"Fortunately, I've never had to prove my manhood. I just have to watch out for nuts who want to use me to prove theirs. How many people did you say you invited to this gathering?"

"Not so many. Maybe a dozen close pals. No one was there that I didn't know personally, if that's what you're getting at."

"What about the person who volunteered Rudy for the magician's trick? Do you know who it was?"

"Oh, that was old Dickie Guttenberg. He's a solid chap, just a joker. Good fun, old Dickie."

Bianca stopped herself from making a rude noise. She made a mental note of good old Dickie Guttenberg's name. "Did this Bey person stick needles in anybody else besides Rudy?"

"Just himself. No other guests."

"Did he use the same needle to pierce Rudy that he used to pierce himself?"

"No, he had a whole case full of needles." Barclay held his index fingers apart about eight inches. "Looked like old-fashioned hatpins."

"When did you become ill?"

Barclay's forehead wrinkled. "That same night that Rudy did, but not nearly as sick, thank goodness. I wondered if it was something we ate at the party, but we were the only two who fell ill afterwards. That I know of, anyway. If Rudy has ulcers, like they say in the papers, maybe whatever it was affected him a lot worse than it did me."

"What did your doctor say is wrong with you, Barclay?"

"The sawbones don't know. A bug of some sort, I reckon. Can't keep anything down. Quite unpleasant. I shan't sully your shell-like ears with the details."

"But you didn't let the fakir stick you?"

Barclay's eyebrows shot up. It hadn't occurred to him that something might have been amiss with the needles. "No. Like I said, no one but Rudy. No needles through the arm for me. That can't be what made me ill."

"Can you think of anything that the two of you did that no one else did, anything that could explain why only you and Rudy fell sick after the party?"

He gave an exaggerated shrug. Bianca could tell that he was becoming annoyed by the implication that something or someone at his party had felled the great Valentino. "No, I don't know what. He didn't eat much that night, but I did. We both drank to excess. He smoked so much I thought he'd set his hair on fire."

"He always has...what?" The look of realization that passed over Barclay's face gave her pause.

"I asked Rudy to give me one of his gaspers. He told me that he has them specially made in Los Angeles with his own favorite

Turkish blend of tobacco. I was curious. It tasted like the gunk at the bottom of a swamp."

Bianca sat up straight. "Did you see anyone else smoke Rudy's cigarettes?"

"I did not. But that doesn't mean that no one else did."

> ~ *Armed with a lead, however slim,*
> *Bianca rushes back to the hospital* ~

Barclay's butler telephoned for a cab to pick Bianca up in the back of the building. Only one clever gal reporter had taken up a vigil at the back entrance. Since Bianca admired female initiative, she gave the woman a brief, if singularly uninformative, statement that since Mr. Warburton was under the weather, she had volunteered to pay a call and give him a personal update on the condition of their mutual friend Mr. Valentino.

"And how is Mr. Valentino?" the reporter asked, as Bianca started toward the waiting cab.

"I only saw him for a minute, but I understand he is doing better." She tossed the answer over her shoulder and firmly closed the taxi door on any more questions.

She glanced at the cabbie's identity plate before sinking back in the seat and putting on her dark glasses. "Take me to the hospital, Mr. Wang." She didn't need to explain which hospital. While Rudolph Valentino was a patient there, there was only one hospital Bianca LaBelle could be interested in.

A light rain had begun to fall as she ran the fan/reporter gauntlet at the main entrance to the Polyclinic and took the elevator to the eighth floor, excited to report the lead she had uncovered.

Beatrice was sitting on the bench outside Rudy's room. She looked up as Bianca stepped off the elevator. Her eyes were red. George was pacing the floor. Bianca paused mid-stride, her news forgotten. "George…" she said. "What is it?"

"Rudy's taken a turn. He has a high fever. The doctor thinks it's pleurisy. They've injected saline into his chest. I don't know what that's supposed to do. I sent a cable to his brother, Alberto, in Italy that he should come to New York as soon as he can."

Bianca sat down heavily on the bench next to Beatrice. "Is it that bad, George?"

"I don't know, but I'm not taking any chances. Alberto should be here."

"Rudy isn't in much pain right now, and he's lucid, in spite of all the drugs," Beatrice said. "Dr. Meeker thinks that's not a good sign. He ought to feel worse than he does."

Bianca heaved a deep sigh. "What do doctors know, Bea? They're all a bunch of quacks."

Beatrice smiled. She knew Bianca was whistling in the dark. "I hope they know what they're doing, honey, at least enough to save his life."

"Can I see him?" Bianca looked to George for guidance, and George gave the uniformed police guard at Rudy's door a questioning glance.

"I have orders that only Mr. Ullman may go in. Miss LaBelle will have to have the doctor's permission." The guard seemed apologetic about having to thwart anyone as beautiful as Bianca.

George opened his mouth to protest, but Bianca put a hand on his arm. "It's all right, George. I want to speak to the doctor anyway."

Bianca had not been raised to put much faith in medical practitioners and had not had reason thus far to be dissuaded from this belief. But Dr. Meeker, the surgeon who had operated on Rudy and was now in charge of his treatment, was a kindly looking man of about fifty who received Bianca in his third-floor office with a sympathetic dignity that she found comforting.

"Miss LaBelle," he said, after offering her a seat before his chart-strewn desk, "Mr. Valentino is in grave condition, I'm afraid, and I do think it best that he be kept quiet and allowed to rest." His voice was soothing. He had much practice in calming hysterical relatives, she thought.

She didn't argue with him. "Doctor, do you have the results of the laboratory tests on Rudy's stomach lining?"

Meeker blinked at her unexpected question. "Miss LaBelle, I would not share the findings without permission if I had. Why do you ask?"

Nothing about Bianca's manner suggested anxiety, but she leaned forward slightly in her chair. "Were you aware that he was pierced completely through his arm with a needle shortly before he collapsed? Could that have had anything to do with his condition?"

"No, I was not aware of that. Mr. Valentino did not mention it, nor did I notice a puncture wound. What are you suggesting?"

Bianca sank back in the chair. "I don't know." She paused, then came out with it. "I'm suggesting poison."

She expected to see an expression of shock on Meeker's face. She was alarmed to note that he only looked thoughtful. The doctor said, "Even if he had been injected with a poison or something equally virulent, on the night he became ill, it wouldn't have anything to do with the ravaged condition of Mr. Valentino's stomach. The perforations and inflammation that I saw would have taken weeks, if not months to develop."

"Doctor, you know that Barclay Warburton took ill on the same night as Rudy, after the party they both attended. No one else that we know of was affected. Barclay told me that Rudy let him have one of his cigarettes, a specially made blend that only Rudy smokes. Could the cigarettes be contaminated with something?"

"Well, if he had been smoking contaminated cigarettes over a long period of time. Something like that could conceivably contribute to the longtime deterioration of his lungs. But his stomach? Unlikely, but not impossible. A cigarette would have to be soaked in a virulent poison to bring on the sudden crisis that Mr. Valentino suffered."

"Doctor, is there any way that you could tell if either the puncture wound or the cigarettes are what brought on Rudy's condition? If there is any sort of test that can tell, please do it. I'll pay for it."

"I understand, Miss LaBelle. Mr. Ullman told me that Mr. Valentino believes someone is trying to do him harm. He also told me that Mr. Valentino has asked you to find out who it is. Mr. Ullman seems to have great faith in your discretion, so I will tell you this. Mr. Valentino has suffered from ulcers for a long time. I believe that tension and unhappiness have greatly contributed to his condition. But something else brought on this crisis, and I am doing everything I can to find out what it was. Everything. Thank you for bringing the puncture wound to my attention. I will examine it. If you can produce one of Mr. Valentino's cigarettes, I'll send it to the lab on the outside chance there is something to your suspicions. Otherwise, I'm afraid that I cannot tell you anything else. If I discover anything untoward, I will inform Mr. Valentino or his representative George Ullman. It will be up to them whether or not to tell you my findings."

Bianca was surprised that George had told the doctor anything about her at all. After she put the bug in Meeker's ear about the needle wound and the cigarettes, she had rather expected to be summarily dismissed from his office for being a self-important, entitled busybody. She took advantage of the doctor's indulgence while she had the chance.

"May I have your permission to see Rudy for a few minutes?"

There was a moment of silence as the doctor considered. He stood up. "I will escort you to his suite. If he is awake and I think he's up to it, you may visit him. Briefly."

Meeker was in Rudy's room for several minutes. Beatrice sat on the bench and twisted her handkerchief. Bianca and George paced the hallway together, deepening the ruts that George had already worn in the floor after more than a week of keeping vigil, while she told him what she had found out from Warburton.

"I'm glad that the doctor knows to look for poison," Bianca said.

"I told him about Rudy's fears right away, even before the operation. I like Meeker. I think that if there's anything unnatural to find, he'll find it."

She didn't have a chance to comment before Meeker emerged and crooked a finger at her. "You may go in, Miss LaBelle. Against my better judgment. He's awake and knows you're here and insists on seeing you. Please don't agitate him."

"Thank you, Doctor." Bianca didn't want to give him time to reconsider. She disappeared into Suite Q.

Meeker turned to George. "I examined the puncture wound Miss LaBelle mentioned. It is barely noticeable, almost completely healed. I took a swab from the area and will have it tested. However, I don't believe it has anything to do with Mr. Valentino's condition."

"Well, I suppose that's good, but now we're right back where we started."

"Miss LaBelle seems to think there's a possibility that Mr. Valentino's custom-made cigarettes may have been poisoned. I cannot imagine that they were, but she was quite adamant, so I told her I would send one to the lab and test for poison. Did he have a cigarette case on him when he came to the hospital?"

George gave the doctor a look that suggested he had lost his mind. "Cigarettes? I certainly wasn't thinking about bringing his cigarettes when I was riding with him in the ambulance. You can't seriously think…"

"Probably not. But given the laboratory results that I've already shared with you, I don't intend to leave any stone unturned."

———

Bianca knew that Rudy had been given large doses of morphine, so she was surprised at how alert he was. In fact, he looked positively at ease, even though his breathing was loud and rasping, like a tin bucket full of rocks, she thought. He smiled at her, and she choked back a sob.

When he spoke, his voice was barely above a whisper. "Did you see Barclay?"

She sat down in the chair beside his bed and took his limp hand. "I did. He gave me some leads, some things to look into, Rudy. We're going to find out what happened, hon. Don't you worry. Don't you worry about a thing. You just get better."

"Everything is going to be all right, now, *cara*. George and I have talked about it. He will take care of everything. We have made all the arrangements."

"Hush, now…"

He interrupted her. "Go back to California, *cara*. Go to Falcon Lair. In my bedroom, in the table next to the bed, there is a drawer that holds my diary. I leave it at home while I am on tour, since I have no time to write. Read it, my darling. In it I wrote everything, all the good and the bad. I have received many death threats and threats of harm, you know, more than just the one I showed you. I wrote about everything in the diary. It is mostly in French. I think you will be able to read it. Your French is good. Also, there are records, letters in my desk in the study. Take whatever you think will help. Give the list to your detective friend."

He seized her wrist and pulled her close. His dark, liquid eyes were wide and stricken. "But there are other things in the diary, all my intimate thoughts. Please do not show anyone—not Natacha, not my brother or sister. Only you. When I am gone, they will make up things about me and I can do nothing about that. Please help me keep something of myself private." He dropped her wrist and managed a wan smile. "And when you read the things I wrote, do not judge me too harshly. Be kind."

"Oh, honey, you could not possibly have secrets as shocking as mine."

His smile widened. "You? How bad could be the secrets of a girl as young as yourself?"

She shook her head. If he only knew. According to the old-time religion of her childhood, there was no atonement severe enough to wipe away her sins. She had broken every commandment, including *thou shalt not kill,* and all before she was out of her teens. And the worst part was that she regretted none of it.

Well, she did regret one transgression. She had dishonored her father and mother and would spend the rest of her life trying to atone for it.

"When you get back to California, go to Falcon Lair," Rudy repeated. "All you need to know of my affairs is there. The answer is there, I'm sure of it."

"Hon, I'm not going anywhere while you're in the hospital."

He gave her hand a weak squeeze. "It won't be long, now, Bianca. You'll be home soon."

When Bianca emerged from the suite, she thrust herself between the doctor and George, interrupting their conversation. She looked desperate. "What can I do, George? What else can I do?"

George cast a look at his wife, who stood and slipped away to find a telephone. He took Bianca by the shoulders. "You're doing all you can. There's nothing else to be done for Rudy. It's all up to him now. Listen, darling, Dr. Meeker took a swab from Rudy's arm, but he says he's almost sure the needle is not what made Rudy sick."

She blinked at George, letting this information sink in. She turned to Meeker. "Almost sure," she repeated.

Meeker nodded. "I can't be one hundred percent sure until I have the swabs tested, but yes, the wound is clean and healing. Something else brought on the crisis."

"The cigarettes, George. Rudy's special cigarettes that he has made for him. Maybe they were poisoned. The doctor could test them. Where are they?"

"I imagine his cigarette box is still back at the hotel."

"I will test them, as I said. Even if they are contaminated some-how, I seriously doubt…" Meeker began, but Bianca interrupted him.

"But what else? What else could it be?"

"It very likely is what it seems to be," Meeker said. "A perfo-rated ulcer, an infection. Pleurisy. The result of years of unhealthy living. He is in extremely critical condition, Miss LaBelle. You must prepare yourself."

"But you will test the cigarettes?"

"I'll send Beatrice to fetch Rudy's cigarette box," George answered for the doctor. "Go back to the hotel, Bianca. There isn't anything else you can do."

"No, Rudy wants me. I can't leave unless there's something for me to do. Something important I can do to help."

George was taken aback by her stubborn insistence. She was on the verge of an uncharacteristic emotional outburst. He knew Bianca LaBelle casually, had met her many times and knew she was one of Rudy's good friends. In his previous experience with her, Bianca was cucumber cool in every situation. Not this girl, with her flushed face and jutting bottom lip. He reminded himself how young she was. If nothing else, her quest to find a nefarious cause for Rudy's illness would keep her busy and out of his hair, and he was grateful for that.

"Darling, Beatrice has gone to telephone Fee, who should be here in a few minutes to take you back to the hotel. Please don't make a scene here in the hall. Rudy would hear it and be upset. Believe me, everything is under control. I promise I'll call you if anything changes."

Bianca drew a breath to argue, her emerald eyes full of indig-nation. But inexplicably, she deflated, an expression crossing her face that George couldn't put his finger on. "All right," she said. "If you swear you'll let me know instantly if there's any change in his condition. Or if the doctor's tests turn up anything. I'll behave, don't worry."

George supposed he should be relieved that she was suddenly so biddable, but he didn't believe it for a second.

Bianca was sitting next to Fee in the back seat of the cab as it pulled out onto West 50th when the mask fell away. "We're not going back to the Ambassador," she said. "We're going to talk to Barclay Warburton again."

Fee snorted. "Why am I not surprised?"

Bianca leaned forward and tapped the cabbie on the shoulder. "Eightieth and Park, and hustle."

> ~ *Her mild tone, insistent, was more frightening*
> *than if she had been shouting.*
> *Barclay knew it was folly to resist her.* ~

Fee plowed through the crowd of reporters to clear Bianca's path at the entrance to Barclay's building. They made it inside the lobby with a minimum number of bumps and bruises, only to be thwarted at Barclay's apartment door by his stalwart butler.

"No, you can't come in. Mr. Warburton is ill. Mr. Warburton is sleeping. What are you doing, you thug? Stop pushing me."

"Barclay! Barclay!" Bianca yelled as Fee jostled their way into the apartment.

Bianca was not leaving, even if Barclay's faithful servant decided to call security to drag her out. (In truth, she was pretty confident that nobody was going to drag her famous ass anywhere.) Fortunately, her confidence was not put to the test, since nobody could sleep through the clamor she was raising. Barclay staggered into the living room, tying the belt of his robe. His bedraggled appearance had not improved in the hour since Bianca had last seen him.

"What the bloody hell? Bianca? Who or what in blazes is that creature with you?"

"Barclay," she said, over top of the butler's restraining arm, "I have to talk to you. Just for a few minutes. I have more questions about the party."

He sagged. "Geeze, I told you everything…"

"The doctor thinks it wasn't the needle, Barclay. And probably not the cigarettes, either. But something happened to him that night. Please…"

"Oh, all right. Let them in, Neil. Bring us some coffee. In fact, make me a toddy while you're at it."

Neil the butler stood aside most unhappily and stalked to the kitchen to do his master's bidding. Barclay waved his uninvited guests toward the couch.

"Did you get to see Rudy?" He began lowering himself into an armchair. "How is he?"

"Barclay, what kind of booze did you serve?" Bianca countered before his behind hit the cushion. "Any moonshine? Who was your supplier?"

Barclay was insulted. "I only serve the highest quality spirits, Bianca, and my supplier is top of the line. On Wednesday night I served champagne. Moët. From Champagne, of course."

"Is that what Rudy drank?"

"Of course."

"Is that all he drank?"

"Well, no. During the magic show I brought out a bottle of single malt whiskey from Iona. Everybody at the table had a shot."

"How many shots did he have?"

"I don't know. More than one, but I didn't keep count. He didn't even finish his last drink. Left it sitting on the table when he went back to the hotel. A waste of expensive… Say… I couldn't stand to see my twenty-five-year-old scotch sitting there all lonely, so after Rudy left, I picked up his glass and slugged down the last of it. Could that be what did us in? Did somebody slip coffin varnish into Rudy's drink?"

"Did you see anybody hovering around the table?"

"Dozens. After all, Valentino was sitting there."

"Who else was at the table?"

"Jean Acker and the Ullmans, Jim Quirk, and myself."

"Did you hire a caterer?"

"No, my own staff waited on us. My longtime *trusted* staff."

"What about Rahman Bey? The doctor doesn't believe that it was the needle that delivered the dose of whatever it was that made Rudy so ill, but was this fakir in a position where he could put something in Rudy's whiskey?"

"Well, he was situated right in front of our table, but he was standing on a makeshift stage that I had brought in."

Bianca's nose prickled, like a bloodhound who's picked up an intriguing scent. "So he called Rudy up on the stage, which left Rudy's drink unattended for a few minutes."

"Yes. But I didn't see…"

She interrupted. "Were you paying attention, Barclay?" She didn't mean to sound accusing. Barclay had been hosting a gathering in his own home. Why would he be looking out for assassins? She apologized for her tone. "I'm just anxious to get to the bottom of this."

Barclay looked mollified, more or less. "No, I wasn't watching Rudy's drink. But now that you mention it, Bey did have an assistant, a stringy little broad in a harem outfit, who kept flitting around the tables when she wasn't handing the magician a prop for his act."

"I suppose it's too much to hope that you kept Rudy's unwashed glass."

Barclay snorted. "I like Rudy, but I don't worship the relics that his lips have touched."

Bianca swiveled on the couch to face Fee. "We need to find this Fakir Rahman Bey."

> ~ *It was no use arguing with Bianca when she was hopped up on adrenaline.* ~

All Barclay knew about the fakir's whereabouts was that the last place he had performed before the party was at the Dalton

Swimming Pool. Barclay's secretary had telephoned the hotel manager, who put him in touch with Bey's agent. Yes, the secretary still had the number. The very much put-upon Neil was persuaded to telephone Bey's secretary, and Bianca left the building with the number of Bey's agent in her purse.

Bianca and Fee went back to the Ambassador to make the telephone call. Bianca would have commandeered Barclay's telephone then and there, but Barclay was fading fast and Neil was becoming more and more belligerent, so Fee persuaded her to make a strategic retreat.

It took nearly an hour to run down the fakir's agent and manager, one Mr. Ismael. By that time Bianca was on the verge of leaping through the lines and pulling the answers she wanted directly out of the poor man's throat.

"Yes, Madame, Mr. Warburton hired the fakir to appear at his party on the evening of August fourteen." Mr. Ismael sounded breathless, as though he couldn't quite get over the fact that he was talking to the great LaBelle. "But only three hours beforehand, Mr. Warburton's servant telephoned to cancel. When Mr. Warburton hired the fakir, he paid with a cheque from the bank, but the next morning, after he canceled, a messenger came to my hotel with double the fee in cash. He said the extra money was for the trouble."

Bianca stood up so quickly she nearly knocked over her chair. "Do you mean to tell me that the fakir never gave a private performance at Barclay Warburton's apartment?"

"No, Madame, he did not."

"Where is Mr. Bey now?"

"He is performing in Atlantic City, Madame. He will return in a week. May I…"

"Thank you, Mr. Ismael. If I need anything else, I will be in touch." She hung up the telephone before the agent could finish his sentence. "Fee, Fee, Fee, did you hear what he said?"

Fee lifted an eyebrow. "Am I a bat, Bianca?"

She was rummaging through her pocketbook and missed the

sarcasm. "I still have the playbill that Barclay gave me. Ah, here it is. Damn, there's no photo of Rahman Bey on the front. But look, here's a drawing inside."

Bianca had resumed her seat at the telephone table. Fee walked over to peer over her shoulder. "You can't tell much from that."

"No. A tall, skinny jobbie in a turban and a nightgown. Looks like long, curly black hair, and skimpy chin whiskers. Listen, George and Beatrice saw whoever it was who impersonated Bey that night. Come, on Fee, we've got to get back to the hospital. I'll bet you anything that the imposter's 'assistant' poisoned Rudy's drink."

Fee wilted at the thought. "Oh, honey, it's late. The Ullmans are probably already back in their room. You've spent the entire day running around like a madwoman. Can't this wait until morning?" As soon as the words were spoken, Fee knew they had fallen on deaf ears. Still, it had to be said.

Bianca was already clicking the receiver to summon the hotel operator. "Hello, call a taxi for me, please. I'll meet him at the back entrance."

> ~ *Life is not like a movie, Bianca.*
> *Everything doesn't turn out all right in the end.* ~

It had begun to spit rain under a darkening sky when Bianca arrived at the hospital. She had insisted that she wanted to go alone, but Fee was just as insistent on coming with her. Bianca's heart dropped as the cab pulled up in front of the Polyclinic. When she had left that afternoon, there were a couple of dozen people milling around the entrance, waiting for news. Now more than a hundred fans and press were holding a vigil outside the hospital.

Bianca turned to Fee in the seat beside her. "What has happened?"

"I don't know any more than you do, sweetheart."

The crowd turned as one to see who had arrived, but there

was no rush to accost the star when she dismounted the cab. The throng parted in eerie silence as she passed. She asked no questions and kept her eyes to herself. She didn't want to know. Her heart was in her throat as she and Fee rode the elevator to the eighth floor.

George was standing in the middle of the hall, waiting for her. "Rudy's in a coma," he said before she could ask.

"I have to talk to you, George," Bianca plowed ahead, pretending she hadn't heard him. "I've found out that the man who entertained at Warburton's party was not Rahman Bey. He was an imposter. I'm almost sure he and his assistant are responsible for poisoning Rudy's drink that night. The doctor has to know right away. Maybe there's time to counteract..."

George interrupted her. "Bianca, the doctor already knows Rudy was poisoned. He knew before you told him."

Bianca blinked at him. "What?"

"His stomach tissues were full of arsenic. They already know, darling, and are treating him aggressively. It's a secret, of course. Please don't be insulted, we would have told you soon, but I think it best that as few people know as possible. We don't want it splashed all over the tabloids."

"But you have to tell the police."

George scoffed. "No, no, no, we don't want the New York police involved. We don't know who to trust."

"I thought this new mayor is trying to clean up the police."

"Oh, Jimmy Walker is a reformer, all right. For a price. No, no police, not yet."

"Does Rudy know what the doctor found?"

"Not for sure. Darling, the doctor thinks that his stomach was in such bad shape that the poison ate right though him like acid."

"But what about the imposter magician?"

"I don't know, Bianca. I think you've uncovered something important. But we'll have to pursue it later. Rudy's in a coma." He repeated himself, not sure she understood.

But she had. "Is he going to die?" She didn't seem upset. She had retreated behind her cool Bianca Dangereuse persona.

"I've sent for a priest," he said as an answer. "It's only a matter of time."

"Let me see him."

"Certainly." George stood aside and she stepped into Rudy's room alone. The guards at the door didn't try to stop her. The two nurses who were seated in wooden chairs beside his bed stood up and moved away to give her some privacy. When she entered, she immediately saw that everything but a small altar and the bed he lay in had been removed from the room. Bianca knelt beside the bed and whispered his name, but he didn't answer. She bent over and kissed his forehead, but he gave no sign that he was aware of her presence. He looked like he was asleep, very peaceful. The red blotches on his face had faded. He was bone thin.

"Rudy," she whispered again, and he stirred. He murmured something in Italian but didn't open his eyes. "Rudy," she said, but he didn't answer. She kissed his forehead. He was cold.

"Miss LaBelle," one of the nurses said. "I'm afraid you must leave now."

Bianca didn't argue. She stood and turned to go.

"Jenny," Rudy said clearly.

Shocked, Bianca turned around. Rudy's eyes were still closed. "Jenny," he said again. "Jenny, Jenny, Jenny."

Bianca walked out into the hall. Her expression was like marble. She said, "Who's Jenny, George?"

George glanced at Fee, who looked stricken. "I don't know," George told her. "I don't know a Jenny. Maybe she's one of his spirit guides."

"Spirit guides. I know that he thinks he has spirit guides. Why didn't he ever talk to me about his spirit guides?"

"He knows you're a skeptic." George was as gentle as possible. "Go back to the hotel with Fee now, darling. In the morning we'll talk about what you discovered. There's nothing more you can do here. Come back tomorrow. You won't be of any help if you're so exhausted you can't see straight."

————

It was nearly ten o'clock when Bianca and Fee got back to the Ambassador. Beatrice shared a cab with them. No one said a word until they bade each other good night in the hall. Bianca did not have the strength to undress. She fell on top of her bed fully clothed. She thought she was too tired to sleep and would spend a long night staring at the shadows on the ceiling, so she was startled when Fee shook her out of unconsciousness. The room was still dark.

"What is it?" she mumbled.

"I'm sorry, honey," Fee said. "That was George on the telephone. Rudy died. I'm sorry."

> ~ *Once broken, a heart*
> *is never quite the same* ~

A light rain was falling just after dawn when Bianca finally made it to Campbell's Funeral Church at Broadway and 66th, where Rudy's body had been taken a few hours earlier. The street in front of the mortuary was packed with people. Mourners, Bianca figured, jammed shoulder to shoulder and refusing to move. So many people, and so soon after Rudy passed. What were they expecting to happen, she wondered? The cabbie inched through the crowd blocking the street, honking his horn incessantly as damp gawkers pressed their faces against the windows to see which celebrity was inside. Bianca stared straight ahead, pointedly avoiding eye contact with altogether-too-festive ghouls who called her name and demanded photos/autographs/kisses. She supposed she should have expected such a thing, but the half-party, half-riot atmosphere frightened her. How was she going to get from the curb to the door of Campbell's without being ripped limb from limb by a mob that professed to love her?

The cab rolled to a stop in front of the funeral home. Bianca was about to tell the cabbie to drive on when three nightstick-wielding cops elbowed their way through the crowd and surrounded her as she dashed inside. She was met in the lobby by Frank Campbell himself, looking equally prosperous and lugubrious in a black suit and tie, his white hair tidily slicked back from his forehead.

"My goodness, there must be thousands of people outside," she said. "How long has this been going on?"

"Ever since Mr. Valentino's remains arrived here at about one this morning. Mr. Ullman has announced that mourners may file through to pay their last respects to Mr. Valentino starting at noon today. People have been gathering ever since."

Rudy would hate this, Bianca thought, thousands of strangers gawking at his body like a sideshow attraction. How could George allow it? She did not offer her opinion. "Where is Mr. Ullman?"

"He left a few minutes ago, but he told me he will return shortly. Please let me escort you to the Gold Room. We've arranged a private viewing room for Mr. Valentino's special friends."

Campbell marched off, unaware that Bianca was not following. She couldn't move. She had not had much of a reaction since Fee told her that Rudy was dead. It didn't seem real, and she was happy to live in denial for a few minutes longer.

Campbell threw a questioning glance over his shoulder when he realized she was not behind him. "Miss LaBelle?"

She braced herself and followed him down the hall. "Who else is here?" She didn't really care, but talking was a small distraction.

"Mr. and Mrs. Ullman just left. Mr. James Quirk is paying his respects right now. Otherwise, you are the first."

Campbell turned and gestured toward the arched entryway to a chapel off the end of the hall. Bianca hesitated, inhaled, then took two purposeful steps into the Gold Room. Rudy lay on a satin-draped bier, a lace pillow under his head. He was dressed in a formal dark suit, his hair beautifully combed and pomaded. His ravaged face was covered with so much makeup that it looked like a mask. A kneeling bench had been placed before the bier, with tall white candles at the head and foot. A forest of fan palms and giant arrangements of flowers stuffed the chapel from floor to ceiling. A bust of the Virgin sat on a plinth at Rudy's head, gazing down at him benignly. Several velvet chairs were arranged in a row before the casket. Bianca sank down onto one of them.

"He doesn't look real, does he?"

Bianca started when Jim Quirk spoke. She hadn't noticed that there was anyone else in the room. Quirk was sitting at the far end of the row. He got up and moved next to Bianca.

"Are you all right, darling?" he said.

Bianca blinked at him. She hadn't considered how she must look. Like the bottom had fallen out of the world, surely. "I'm all right. Stunned, I guess. I thought he'd pull through."

"We all did. I was outside the hospital when he died, you know. They brought out his body in a basket."

"A basket?"

"A big coffin-shaped wicker basket." He folded his arms across his chest, a thoughtful expression on his face.

"How is George holding up? I haven't talked to him since Rudy…" She couldn't say the word.

"Somber, of course, but holding up well. He has a lot to do. Rudy's brother, Alberto, is on his way here from Italy. Rudy named George as the executor of his estate. He's making all the arrangements."

"Why is George going to let the public gawk at him? Rudy would never go for that."

"I'm guessing it was Campbell's idea and George bought it. Free publicity, you know."

Bianca sagged. "Oh, Jimmy. If I die while I'm still famous, I'm going to have Fee bury an empty coffin with my name on it and then smuggle my body back to my family in secret."

"I won't tell if you'll tell me where your family is, first."

"Forget it. By the way, I read your profile of Rudy and me in *Photoplay*. Nice job."

"Thanks. Will you sit down with me soon for another interview?"

"Shut up, Jimmy. I'm not here to talk business."

"Of course not. I'm sorry. He looks terrible, doesn't he? Not like himself at all."

In truth Bianca had been avoiding a close look at the body. She stood up for a better view. Quirk was right. Rudy looked terrible, waxy and unreal. But Bianca had seen an inordinate number of dead bodies in her short life, and none of them had resembled their living selves. Her vision blurred as her eyes flooded with tears. "Oh, Rudy," she sighed.

Quirk appeared at her side. "You saw him last night?"

"I did. He wasn't conscious, but he was talking."

"What about?"

She shot Quirk a poisonous look. "Quit working for five minutes, will you?"

He seemed shocked at the accusation. "I'm not. I mean, it's just that…"

"Just what?"

"There's something strange going on here, Bianca. Rudy didn't die a natural death, did he?"

Bianca sat down heavily. What on earth was she going to say to that? James Quirk may have been Rudy's friend, but he was a Hollywood journalist and the managing editor of *Photoplay*. Yet he knew everyone who was anyone—who was feuding, screwing around, going broke, breaking the law. Could he help in her quest to find out who murdered Rudy? Could she trust him?

She'd have to think about that. Trusting the wrong people had gotten her into trouble before. "Talk to me after the funeral,

Jimmy." He seemed satisfied with her sort-of answer. He handed her his pocket square and she wiped her eyes. A smear of dark mascara came off on the handkerchief. "Oh, Lord, I must look a mess."

He patted her hand. "You look lovely, Bianca."

"You're a liar, Jimmy Quirk, but thanks."

Private detective Ted Oliver made the long drive from Santa Monica, through Los Angeles, to the foothills outside of Pasadena for his weekly meeting at the estate-cum-fortress of mobster K. D. Dix, in order to deliver the weekly progress report on his investigation into the mysterious death of one Graham Peyton.

K. D. Dix was a small, plump, elderly woman with white hair and round, rosy cheeks. She was charming and motherly, always cheerful, it seemed. One would never know to meet her that she was the *capo* of a vast crime empire and a cold-blooded killer.

A few months earlier, in February of 1926, a violent Pacific storm off the Southern California coast had uncovered a human skeleton, buried for years under a rockslide at the foot of the Pacific Palisades, near Oliver's apartment in Santa Monica. The unfortunate mug whose bones were unearthed had once been Graham Peyton, a notorious grifter, bootlegger, dope peddler, and seducer of innocent young women. Peyton had been on Dix's payroll when he disappeared five years earlier, along with fifty thousand dollars. Dix wanted to know how his bones had ended up on the beach and who had been responsible for putting them there.

When he had agreed to take on the job, lured by the promise of a big payday, Oliver was under the impression that Peyton had been a low-level syndicate operative who thought he could get away with skimming a little off the top and had been bumped off by some other thug for the money. A classic double-double cross. No big loss to humanity. No one should have cared about the death of such an unsavory character. But as it turned out, K. D. Dix cared very much.

Graham Peyton was her son.

Oliver always tried to stick as close to the truth as possible when he talked to Dix, since she was not forgiving of lies. But there was one very large truth that he avoided mentioning at all.

The beloved actress Bianca LaBelle, née Blanche Tucker of Boynton, Oklahoma, and Dix's son, Graham Peyton, had had quite a history before Peyton disappeared off the face of the earth and Bianca became one of the most famous women in the world. Bianca had told him so herself.

His life was not his own anymore, but his thoughts were still private—at least until the dreaded day when Dix would finally lose patience with his failure to deliver Peyton's killer and order one of her enforcers to crush his thumbs in a vise. If and when that happened, Oliver feared that he would spill everything he knew about Bianca LaBelle and Graham Peyton, whether Dix asked him about it or not.

Dix had rubbed out a lot of people in her time—some in

revenge for her son's death, some for thinking they could cross her, some simply in the course of business or on general principal—and Oliver had a gnawing premonition that one of these days he was going to be one of them. Because he suspected he had already figured out who killed Graham Peyton, and if he could manage to avoid it, he had no intention of telling Dix.

The question now was how long was he going to be able to keep his boss off Bianca's trail, keep himself alive, and keep Dix from hurting someone he was beginning to care very much about? It didn't matter to him that Bianca LaBelle was a star of the silver screen and he was a lowly gumshoe who had eked out a living by getting the goods on cheating spouses—until he had gotten himself mixed up with a murderous lady gangster.

Oliver had been at this investigation for over six months, and he didn't know how much longer his nerves were going to be able to take the constant dread and outright fear that ate at him every waking moment and invaded his dreams.

Oliver hated these meetings.

Every week, he dutifully gave Dix the rundown on all the records he had checked, all the people he had questioned, all the information he had gathered, and all the progress he had not made. He had told her from the beginning that the likelihood of his unearthing her son's murderer after all this time was slim to none. But his digging had uncovered treason from other quarters within Dix's organization. She had never suspected that Mr. Ruhl, her second-in-command for over thirty years, was stealing from her until Oliver unmasked him, so she insisted that he carry on. K. D. Dix was not a woman to be crossed. Dix had an army of goons to do her bidding, but she was not averse to doing her own dirty work. A small, elderly woman could usually get close enough to an unsuspecting schlub to throw acid in a face or shove a shiv into a carotid artery. She also knew an excellent never-fail recipe for concrete overshoes.

When Oliver met with Dix in her comfy Edwardian parlor, he

made it a point to sit on the couch farthest from her throne-like leather wingback chair. As a bonus, this gave him a clear view of Dix's latest bodyguard, Juan, who hovered in the corner like a menacing shadow and said nothing. Oliver didn't know if the man's name was actually Juan, since Dix had never introduced him or even acknowledged his presence, but his black hair and brooding black eyes gave him a Latin look, so Oliver figured Juan was as good a handle as any. After a while Oliver hardly noticed him in the corner any more than he noticed the floor lamps.

Dix poured the tea herself out of a silver service into delicate china cups. The pastries, artfully arranged on a chinoiserie tray, looked delectable. After all, most of Dix's pleasure establishments were fronted by bakeries. But Oliver was never able to choke down any of the little cakes. After she was done with him, Dix would wrap up a few petit fours in brown paper and insist that he take them home. He usually handed them to someone on the street when he got back to Santa Monica.

But today, just as he was making a move to stand, so near his escape, Dix said, "Hold on, Ted. There's something else I want to talk to you about."

Oliver said nothing, watching Dix in silence as she finished her tea, waiting for her to enlighten him. K. D. Dix was no longer the gorgeous little firecracker from San Francisco who had freed herself from a violent pimp by means of a Colt .44, but age had not dimmed the ice and fire in her blue eyes.

"Have you been following the news about Rudolph Valentino's death?"

Oliver's forehead wrinkled. An odd thing for Dix to bring up. "How could I not? It's all over the papers. Especially since they brought his body back here to Los Angeles for burial." He had actually met Valentino briefly, at Bianca LaBelle's house. But he wasn't going to tell Dix that.

"I want you to take a recess from investigating Graham's death and look into it for me. In the past few months, I've been hearing whispers that there was a plot to get rid of him. I didn't put much credence in the rumor. Hollywood is rife with rumors. But now..." Her voice trailed off and she sighed.

"You think somebody offed Valentino?" He almost added, "Why do you care?" but caught himself in time.

She got the gist anyway. "You needn't look so skeptical. You don't need to know the details, either. My associate in New York tells me that Valentino's doctor tested him for poison and found a lethal dose of arsenic in his tissues."

"You want me to go to New York?"

"That won't be necessary. I already have operatives in New York, but I don't think the answer is back there. I have a job for you here in California." She placed her teacup on the side table and folded her hands in her lap. "What do you know about Tony Cornero?"

Oliver flopped back down on the couch. "Tony the Hat. He owns a fleet of freighters and smuggles Canadian whiskey into Southern California. He anchors his ships off the coast and unloads the liquor into speedboats to bring it to the beaches, where trucks pick it up and distribute the goods to his customers."

She nodded. "Tony has come up with an ingenious new sideline. He's converted one of his freighters into a casino and christened it the *Monaco*. It's anchored off the coast beyond the three-mile limit. Cornero ferries the high and mighty out for an evening of gambling and debauchery beyond the reach of the law. It's only been going on for a few months. It's an experiment, but I hear it's turned out to be quite a lucrative one."

"A high-class gambling joint just outside of U.S. jurisdiction. That shows a lot of ingenuity. I'm surprised that no one has thought of it before."

"Look into Tony's business dealings. I'd like to know who his backers are, if any."

"I doubt if he needs backers. The guy's a millionaire. In fact..." Oliver didn't finish the thought. It would be right up Dix's alley to muscle Cornero out and take over his operation. All she needed to know was who she'd have to eliminate in order to do it. "How does this figure in with Valentino?"

"Rumor is the Chicago outfit is trying to expand their territory onto the West Coast and has been making overtures to Cornero. My inside man tells me that Valentino was involved somehow, maybe as an investor, but I don't have any solid information. There will be a memorial service for him in Hollywood on the fourteenth. I want you to be there, see if anybody interesting shows up, anybody from Chicago or New York."

Oliver nodded. Capone and his cohorts had been interested in expanding their business onto the West Coast for years. Southern California had plenty of homegrown organized crime of its own, so Dix and her ilk wouldn't appreciate the competition. He stood up again. "I'll see what I can find out."

> ~ *Embroiled in a battle he can never win,*
> *Oliver wonders how he can quit the field.* ~

Oliver parked his roadster by the side of the coast highway below Santa Monica and sat down in the sand to watch the sun set over the Pacific. It always took a long time for his heart rate to return to normal after these meetings with Dix.

Oliver didn't see anyone on the beach, but he suspected that he had been followed. K. D. Dix, the most ruthless—and most unlikely—mobster on the West Coast, kept a close eye on her hired hands. Oliver didn't care if he was being tailed. Let Dix's goons gawk at him all they wanted. In fact, maybe he'd sit here until tomorrow, just to torture whoever was watching him.

Oliver sat on the sand for hours, until the sun was well down, bleaching the color out of the sky, wondering about the real reason K. D. Dix cared a fig about the death of Valentino. So what if he was connected to Tony the Hat?

It was already quite dark by the time he parked his roadster on the street in front of his building in Santa Monica and trudged up the stairs to his one-bedroom flat above a clothier.

Someone was sitting on the stairs in the dark stairwell. Oliver pressed himself to the wall at the landing and slipped his hand inside his jacket to grip the handle of the .38 in his shoulder holster.

"Who's there?" he said.

"Is that Mr. Oliver?" The voice that answered sounded like it belonged to a kid.

Oliver let out a breath. He hadn't realized he was holding it. "Who wants to know?"

The figure stood up, a dark shape at the top of the gloomy stairwell. "Western Union, sir." He walked down the stairs and into the weak yellow light coming from the single bulb hanging from the ceiling over the landing. He was a kid all right, maybe fourteen. Too young for facial hair but old enough to have a bad complexion. He was dressed in a gray Western Union uniform.

He held out an envelope with Oliver's name printed on the front.

Oliver took it. "Why didn't you just shove it under the door?"

"I was told to put it into your hand, sir."

Besides, you wouldn't have gotten a tip, Oliver thought, as he dug through his pockets for a coin to give the boy.

The courier gave him a saucy grin as he pocketed the quarter and bounded down the stairs. Oliver stared at the envelope for a minute and sighed. Well, no use to stand out here on the landing. Whatever the news was, it wasn't going to get any better with time.

He paused before he put the key in the lock. He did that a lot these days, taking a second to steel himself for any surprises that might be waiting for him behind the door. Just because a guy is paranoid doesn't mean somebody isn't out to get him.

The apartment was so dark that he had to rely on his familiarity with the layout to stumble across the floor to the table lamp and flip it on. Either everything was as he had left it or whoever had searched the place had not bothered to tidy up Oliver's mess in the process.

He walked into the kitchen and laid the envelope on the table, then removed his tie and poured himself a stiff drink before he sat down. He ran a finger under the sealed flap, withdrew the telegram, took a slug of gin, and began to read.

NEED YOUR HELP *STOP* GO TO MY HOUSE TOMORROW AT 7:00 A.M. *STOP* THEY'LL BE EXPECTING YOU AT GATE *STOP* SEE THAT YOU'RE NOT FOLLOWED *STOP* BL

He absently lowered his glass to the tabletop. "Aw, shit," he murmured. He hadn't seen Bianca LaBelle in months, not since he had questioned her about her connection to Graham Peyton. He hadn't expected to ever see her again, really. They didn't run in the same circles. In fact, last he heard, she had gone to New York, same as a dozen other luminaries, to maintain a vigil at Valentino's bedside. The late star's body had arrived in Los Angeles yesterday. Bianca had probably come back to town on the same train.

When Oliver met Valentino at Bianca's house during—what else—a party, the actor had struck him as a dark, perfectly put-together presence with an intense gaze. At the time, Oliver only had eyes for Bianca, so his memory could be faulty.

What could she possibly want from him? He didn't need any more complications in his life right now. That didn't mean he wasn't going to drive to Beverly Hills tomorrow to meet with her.

> ~ *It Can't be a Coincidence,*
> *so Maybe it's a Conspiracy.* ~

There was a new guard at the iron gate that separated LaBelle's estate, Orange Garden, from the rest of the world. Oliver gave his name, and the guard seemed surprised to actually find him on the admittance list. Bianca LaBelle probably didn't get many visitors who drove rattletraps and wore off-the-rack suits. He parked his Ford in the circular drive in front of the house and made his way to the front door. The huge, carved wooden entryway to Bianca's mansion made Oliver feel like he was a Visigoth demanding entry at the massive gates of Rome, and just about as welcome.

It took a few minutes for Bianca's snippy maid, Norah, to appear and crack open the door enough for him to slide into the foyer.

Norah was a rather pretty woman, but she always looked like she smelled something a little bit off. Of course, that could just be him.

"What's this all about?" he said.

Norah took his hat. "Miss LaBelle wants to talk to you." She started walking toward the living area without looking to see if Oliver was following.

"How long has she been back from New York?"

"Just since last night. She came back on Mr. Valentino's funeral train."

Last night? She must have sent the telegram to him during one of the train's layovers. "Can you give me a hint about what she wants?"

"I really don't know, Mr. Oliver."

Norah led him into an office off the cavernous living room. He had never been in this room before. He expected that he could visit a different room every day for a month before he saw them all.

This office unmistakably belonged to someone in the motion picture business. One wall was lined with film canisters. A projector stood in a corner. A large but unglamorous wooden desk sat under the bank of windows that looked out onto the pebbled deck and the swimming pool. The desktop was neat, containing only a blotter, some fountain pens, and a pile of scripts. And a telephone, one of those new kinds with a cradle on top to hold the receiver.

"Have a seat, Mr. Oliver." Norah hung his hat on a rack beside the door and gestured to the leather chair in front of the desk. She pointedly looked at the clock on the wall. Ten minutes to seven. "Can I bring you anything? Coffee?"

"Just some water, thanks."

"Miss LaBelle is on a telephone call to New York." Norah paused, making sure he was properly impressed. He was, and not just because the call was coming from three time zones away. A long-distance trunk call from New York to Los Angeles cost more than fifteen dollars for three minutes and God knew how much for each minute thereafter. Norah continued, "Please wait here. She'll be in shortly. In the meantime, please don't touch anything."

Oliver sank back into the upholstery and folded his hands over his stomach. "Don't worry, doll. I'll be good."

The minute Norah closed the door, Oliver pulled the pile of scripts toward himself and rifled through them. Only two were treatments for new Dangereuse flicks. The remaining five or six were all over the map. *Helen of Troy.* Yeah, Oliver could see it. *The Blue Parrot. Something Happened.* That one was a comedy. The proposed male lead was that English guy Ronald Colman. Had Bianca ever done a comedy? Most of the Dangereuse movies had some laughs in them. She'd probably be really good in a comedy.

He pushed the pile back to the corner when he heard Norah fiddling with the knob, then stood to relieve her of the tray she was carrying. A glass, a carafe of water. A couple of cookies.

He had just lifted one of the cookies to his mouth when the door opened and Bianca walked in. She was clad in a black, drop-waist linen dress with a gray-and-white-patterned inset in the elbow-length sleeves and a scarf of the same pattern tied around her hips. Her remarkable green eyes were enhanced by a smoky gray shadow and delicately outlined with kohl.

He had thought he was prepared, but every time he saw her

in the flesh, he was stunned. Nobody could be that gorgeous in real life. The cookie ended up in his lap, then slid onto the floor when he stood up.

If she was aware of his awe, she didn't show it. She waved him back down and pulled a side chair up to the desk beside him. "Thank you for coming, Mr. Oliver. I need a favor. Do you think you could get away from Dix long enough to look into something for me? I hope it won't take long. I'll pay you, of course."

"It depends. What do you have in mind?"

"I want you to help me look into Rudy's death." The look of shock on his face must have been apparent, for she hesitated. "What's wrong? You surely know my friend Rudy Valentino died."

Oliver recovered quickly. "I don't live under a rock. You surprised me is all. Why do you want to look into it? The papers said he died of peritonitis."

"I'm telling you different. I believe it was murder. And I expect you to keep that to yourself, Mr. Oliver."

"What makes you think he was murdered?"

"Last July, while Rudy and I were finishing our movie…"

Oliver interrupted her. "You and Valentino did a movie together?"

Bianca slid him an incredulous side glance. Was he joking? Did he not read the trade publications? She thought everyone in the world knew that LaBelle and Valentino were finally going to be on the screen together. Oliver's expression was perfectly sincere, and Bianca almost laughed aloud—not at Oliver, but at herself. For a moment she had forgotten that the motion picture industry was not the center of the universe and neither were she and Rudy.

"Yes, it's called *Grand Obsession*. It's set to be released early next year. We were supposed to go on tour together…" A welling of emotion caught her off guard as it dawned on her that that would not happen now that Rudy was truly gone. She swallowed down the lump in her throat. "…next January, after I wrapped this new *Dangereuse* I'm working on and he was finished with the *Son of the Sheik* tour."

"Wow, a flick with the two of you will make a wad of money. Especially now that…" He hesitated when he saw that finishing his observation would distress Bianca. He started over. "Will you still have to do the tour on your own?"

Bianca looked down at her tightly clutched hands. She relaxed her fingers with an effort and placed her hands loosely in her lap. "Probably with more appearances now than ever," she admitted, then sternly forced herself to return to business. "While we were still shooting *Obsession*, Rudy told me that somebody was out to get him. He showed me a note that someone left in his dressing room. It said, 'Valentino will die.' And then he did."

Oliver leaned forward and perched one elbow on the desktop. "I imagine that people as famous as you and Valentino get notes and letters from wackadoos all the time."

"True. But what you don't know is that Rudy was poisoned. He knew it, too. The doctor said it was arsenic, administered in a massive dose that ate right through him. I'm almost sure a fake magician and his fake assistant were hired to doctor his drink during a party he attended on the night he collapsed."

So it was true! Oliver tried not to look too interested. "I didn't read anything about that."

"No, his manager is keeping the whole thing under wraps. But I promised Rudy that I'd find out who poisoned him, and I will, no matter how long it takes. That night the imposter magician stuck a needle Rudy's his arm as part of his magic act, and at first I thought that had to be what killed him—something on the needle. But the doc said the needle wound was clean and it had to be something he ate or drank." She filled Oliver in on the imposter Rahman Bey and his ersatz assistant and her suspicion that Rudy's drink was poisoned at Barclay Warburton's party.

"I did everything I knew to find out who the imposters were or who hired them, called in every favor I was ever owed by everyone

I could think of on the East Coast. *Bupkis,* as Alma would say. But I'm no investigator. Not to mention that I can't cross the street without drawing a crowd, so I need your help. Your *discreet* help."

He leaned back into the leather chair, still trying to digest the fact that in the space of a day two women had put him on the same case. Two women he could not resist for totally different reasons. "What do you have in mind?"

"I want you to go to Rudy's burial next week, see who shows up. See if you can see anything or anybody suspicious."

"I think I can wrangle an invitation."

"I'll get you an invitation," Bianca said. "I've already told his agent that I'm asking you to come. The memorial service is going to be at the Church of the Good Shepherd on the fourteenth, and afterward, they'll take his body to Hollywood Memorial Park for interment."

"What or who am I looking for? Did he give you any names, anybody he was suspicious of or any idea who might have had it in for him? Anything I can sink my teeth into?"

"Rudy gave me two or three leads. He's had some trouble with some bad people, gambling debts and the like. Also, he thought maybe the Black Hand or the Fascisti had it in for him."

"Yeah, I know of the Black Hand. A loose bunch of mobsters, Italians, mostly. Blackmailers. But they've been pretty much muscled out by organized crime in the past few years. But the Fascists? What could any Italian have against Valentino? I'd think he'd be their hero, being Italian himself and all."

"Mussolini thinks he's a traitor to Italy because he applied for American citizenship. Rudy told me that his films have been banned in Italy. The weird thing is that while Rudy's body lay in state in New York, a bunch of thugs in black shirts calling themselves the Fascisti League of North America muscled into the funeral home and stood like an honor guard beside the coffin for a whole day. They brought this huge wreath of flowers with a blue satin ribbon that said 'From Benito Mussolini.' Could that be some sort of sinister message, a taunt? Anyway, I'm hoping that you can take advantage of your mob ties—or perhaps I should say mob acquaintances—and see if you can find out anything. I'll pay you well."

Oliver tried his best to keep his expression neutral. This was almost the same job that Dix had given him, except, of course, Dix had named the mobsters she wanted him to investigate. He was going to have to approach this cautiously. He didn't want Dix to know that Bianca was on the same warpath. "You're saying you want me to ask Dix if she knows anything? Believe me, you don't want K. D. Dix to spare you a single thought. Besides, she told me in no uncertain terms that until I find out who killed her son, I work exclusively for her."

"I don't particularly want Dix thinking about me, either. She doesn't have to know I'm involved. In fact, you don't have to bring it up with her at all. There must be other people in her organization you can talk to. Make some discreet inquiries. Can you manage that without her finding out? If there's anything to the mob connection, surely there're whispers about it in the underground."

"Well, Valentino's death is big news, so I can ask around, you know, curious-like." As he spoke, he had a nagging feeling that Bianca being involved in any way with this unsavory business was asking for trouble. He also knew he'd do anything he could to help her. He had realized that after he felt a stab of disappointment that she had called him Mr. Oliver instead of Ted.

"Nose around this Black Hand connection, will you? I'll have more leads for you soon. I'm going to Falcon Lair as soon as you leave and retrieve some of Rudy's papers before anyone else can get to them."

"Falcon Lair. Valentino's place up the hill? Won't the servants object to your snooping around?"

She was surprised that he would ask. "Of course not. They all know me. I've already made arrangements for Luther—he's the caretaker—to let me in. As a matter of fact, why don't you come with me? You may recognize something significant that I wouldn't."

She was right, and he was tempted. But he couldn't take the chance that Dix would learn that they had been seen together at Valentino's estate. "I think it'd be better if you go by yourself. I want to dig into the Italian connection first. And listen, when I do go to the burial, pretend you don't know me. Don't draw any attention to me. I'd like to eyeball the crowd, see if anybody stands out, and I'll learn more if I'm invisible."

She didn't question him. "All right. I'll let you know if I find something interesting in Rudy's papers." She stood. He was being dismissed.

He stood, too, grabbed his hat from the tree and put it on. "By the way, I'm sorry about Valentino. He seemed like a nice guy. I know you were friends."

She smiled. He had said the right thing. "Thank you. We were."

"I read about the funeral they had for him in New York. Sounds like it was a circus."

Bianca groaned. "It was pandemonium. Women were fainting in the streets. Some girl even tried to kill herself in front of the mortuary. A bunch of ghouls pretending to be mourners stole all the flowers off his bier and cut hunks out of the draperies. The funeral itself was horrible. Pola...that's Pola Negri. She and Rudy had been dating. Anyway, Pola finally got to New York after Rudy died, just in time for the funeral. She made a spectacle of herself, screaming and fainting and weeping. She had a big floral arrangement made for his casket that spelled out her name with red flowers. The press loved it. She told everybody that she and Rudy were engaged, and I know for a fact that that's a flat-out lie. She made it all about her." Bianca turned white with indignation as she recounted the tale. Her hands were clutched into fists.

"Mary Pickford kept telling me that Pola was probably really grief-stricken, that Europeans don't believe in hiding their feelings.

But I think Mary was just trying to keep me from strangling Pola. Before Rudy died, I thought she really cared for him, but now I think she was using him. What Pola loves is the camera. When she finally made it to New York, she brought her publicist with her. Anyway, I'll bet money that she makes a big scene at the burial next week, so don't be surprised at her histrionics. The train trip back here was horrible, too. There was a morbid crowd and film crews at every stop. People kept trying to force their way onto the train. As we got close to Los Angeles, we heard that there were thousands of people waiting at the railroad depot downtown, so we decided to stop in El Sereno and secretly take his body the rest of the way to the undertaker's in a hearse. And I have to live through another extravaganza when they bury him next week. At least the burial is invitation only."

Oliver's expression must have conveyed sympathy, for Bianca abruptly stopped talking and stood up. She walked to the window and stood with her back to him for a moment, regaining her composure.

Oliver sighed. "I'll start asking around about Valentino's affairs, Bianca. Send the funeral invitation to me by messenger. I'll see what I can dig up about any local Black Hand activity, and in the meantime, if you learn anything helpful at Falcon Lair, let me know."

She turned around to face him, her marble facade restored. "Thank you, Mr. Oliver."

~ *High on the Mountain,*
Bianca alights on Falcon Lair ~

Bianca saddled her favorite mount, a little sorrel quarter horse mare with two white stockings on her front legs and a white muzzle that made her look like she had been drinking milk. The area above Beverly Hills was crisscrossed with bridle paths, and most of the wealthy estate owners kept thoroughbreds or tall

American saddlebred horses. Bianca had one of each herself and loved them. But she was partial to her sturdy, brainy Peach. Peach reminded her of the horses she had first learned to ride when she was growing up in Oklahoma. She favored a Western saddle when she rode Peach. An aristocratic English saddle did not suit such a practical, no-nonsense creature.

Rudy's caretaker, Luther Mahony, had warned Bianca that once she turned north off San Ysidro onto Benedict Canyon Drive, she would be passing a parade of sightseers on their way to Falcon Lair, some on foot, some in autos. Perhaps even an omnibus or two. She had no desire to become part of the show. The road was narrow, so there was no way she would be able to keep her distance from the mourners' autos. The best she could do was disguise herself and keep moving as fast as she could, hoping the gawkers could not get a good look at her when she passed.

If anyone recognized her as she passed car after car inching up the hill, she did not stick around long enough to know about it. She turned off the long, winding road onto Bella Drive, past the gates of screenwriter Frances Marion's mansion and on to the top of the knoll to Rudy's white, rough-plastered house with its tall gate of Italian grillwork. A spectacular view of the city of Los Angeles spread out below.

Rudy and Natacha had bought the house together back in '24 and named it Falcon Lair, after the historical epic they planned to make called *The Hooded Falcon*, based on the life of Rodrigo Diaz, the Spanish hero El Cid. Falcon Lair was a two-story Spanish Colonial villa with stucco walls, a central turret, and a red-tile roof. It sat on an eight-acre lot with stables, kennels, a multi-car garage, and a separate house for the servants.

The Hooded Falcon was never made. The production deal fell through, as did Rudy and Natacha's marriage. Rudy moved into Falcon Lair alone and renovated it to suit himself. He had planned the landscaping and planting of the gardens, outlining the entire property with stately Italian cypress trees. A beautiful

Spanish-style fountain sat in the courtyard, just in front of the oak entry doors decorated with carved Roman horsemen.

Luther was waiting for her at the back gate. He took charge of Peach and let Bianca into the house through a side door that couldn't be seen from the road.

Rather than head directly into the master bedroom, she spent half an hour wandering through the empty house. So empty, now that Rudy was gone forever. She had always considered the decor too busy for her taste, but it suited Rudy to a tee. He had always been a collector of rare and beautiful artifacts, and had turned his home into a replica of a medieval castle, with grand fireplaces and a wood-beamed ceiling, the walls covered with ancient weaponry and renaissance portraits.

Where to start? She was impressed by the range of subjects on his bookshelf: rare first editions, classical and modern literature in one, two, three…she counted five separate languages. Rudy might have been a matinee idol, but he was no dummy. A photograph of Rudy as Ahmed ben Hassan, the character he played in *The Sheik*, sat in a gilt frame on a side table. The part that had made him famous. Well, not just famous. *The Four Horsemen of the Apocalypse* had made him famous. *The Sheik* had vaulted him into the stratosphere. She picked up the photo and studied it for a moment. She was a mildly surprised that he kept it on display. He had never made a secret of the fact that he was not happy with his own acting in that picture. Still, he had told her that shooting the movie was a lot of fun, with plenty of action and horsemanship, which he loved. Oxnard and Santa Barbara had doubled for Arabia, and the crew had pitched tents and camped out on the dunes for weeks, gathering around campfires at night and singing to the accompaniment of Rudy's guitar. He and Natacha were together by then, and the world was his oyster.

She perused the bookshelf carefully, looking for anomalies. She kept many of her own secrets on the bookshelf in her library, books and papers that she would rather no one else see, like her diary and financial statements, and a few other perhaps less-than-legal documents, hidden in plain sight. But Rudy apparently did not subscribe to her philosophy. As interesting as his library was, she found no clues to who would want to kill him.

On the wall beside the bookshelf hung a giant portrait of Rudy as Julio Desnoyers, his breakout role in *The Four Horsemen of the Apocalypse*, dressed in boots and gaucho pants, one hand upon his hip, his dark eyes gazing directly at the viewer. On a small table to the right of the portrait sat the hand. Several years earlier, an artist had carved a life-sized sculpture of one of Rudy's hands out of alabaster. It was a fine, sensitive hand, Bianca thought, lying relaxed, palm open, on a block of black marble.

She touched it, slid her own hand into it, transported back to the day he had taught her to dance the tango.

That had been Alma's idea.

Alma Bolding had engaged teachers of all kinds to help turn the naive teenaged refugee Blanche Tucker into elegant, sophisticated Bianca LaBelle—acting, French language, economics, art and music, elocution, even Eastern philosophy and Japanese self-defense. And dancing.

Bianca was still living at Alma's Hollywood Hills mansion at the time and was in the middle of shooting *The Golden Goblet*, her very first Bianca Dangereuse picture, unaware that she was about to become a star. Alma had swept into the breakfast room one morning with her silk dressing gown billowing behind her and announced, "I know the perfect person to teach you the tango, darling. Remember that delicious, sloe-eyed young Italian who was here with Natacha Rambova last week? Well, I just saw his new flick. He plays an Argentine playboy, and he did the most sensual, dripping-with-sex-appeal tango..."

"You mean Rudolph Valentino?" Bianca was amused that Alma assumed she didn't know who Rudy was. Alma was so self-absorbed that she barely knew anyone else existed. "His *Four*

Horsemen movie is a big hit. I seriously doubt he's looking to give dance lessons, Alma."

Alma made a dismissive gesture with one hand while pouring coffee with the other. "Pooh, darling. I'm sure he'll do it for me. Constance Talmadge tells me he used to give dance lessons when he first came to America, and she thinks he's the best dancer she's ever seen. After all, we want only the best instructors for you, or what's the point of taking lessons?"

Bianca had shot a knowing glance at Alma's friend, business manager, and housekeeper Mrs. Gilbert, who was sitting next to her at the table, quietly sipping orange juice and keeping her opinion to herself. Alma was an irresistible force, at least in her own mind, so there was no use arguing with her.

But much to Bianca's amazement, Rudy had agreed. He had not yet begun shooting *The Sheik*, and she had not wrapped *The Golden Goblet*. They were both still trembling on the edge of celebrity. The first evening he came to Alma's house, Bianca asked him why on earth he would agree to give dance lessons to an unknown, teenaged, aspiring actress. Surely he didn't need the money. Did Alma have something on him?

He had laughed. "No, *cara*. I am not doing this for money. You and I had such a nice talk at Alma's party, and I wanted to get to know you better. I think you will soon be a very great success."

Bianca was as enchanted by his dark good looks and his old-world charm as every other woman in the world, but his unexpected praise had immediately put her on her guard. She had been fooled by a smooth-talker once before and she had no intention of falling for it again.

They only had three sessions before their schedules intervened and put an end to his visits, but he was a wonderful teacher. He was warm and funny and respectful, but then the dance would begin, and he would pull her so close that their bodies melded before he swept her around the room. After the lesson he would kiss her hand and leave to walk down the hill to his own house, and she'd rush into Alma's backyard and jump into the swimming pool to cool off. It took her a while to realize that she didn't have to hold herself aloof from Rudy. He had no intention of seducing her. Years later, he admitted that he was as daunted by her as she had been by him. Neither had realized their own allure back in those days.

Bianca felt tears prickle as she relived the memory. What good friends they had become, and yet, now that he was gone, she was sorry that she had never let it become more than that.

Why do you never love? he had asked her. Ever since Graham Peyton, she had not allowed herself to get close to anybody. If she had expressed the slightest interest, would Rudy have responded? She would never know now.

His study proved more promising ground to search. She removed piles of papers from his desk drawers and leafed through them. Many of the papers were in Italian. The only ones she could figure out were letters from his sister in Italy. She had a smattering of Italian, but not enough. She'd have to have help translating them, if she could find an Italian-speaker she could trust to keep his mouth shut. There were letters from France, also, mostly from friends. She could manage those on her own. Some had letterheads from Parisian art dealers. But there were plenty in English, as well. Bills for jewelry, clothing from London, antique Spanish furniture, rare wines and liquor. Payments to and invoices from the contractors working on the house and grounds. Cars. Veterinary bills. She had known Rudy was a profligate spender, but yikes! She stuffed the more interesting papers into a knapsack to take home and peruse at her leisure.

She finally went into his bedroom and sat down on the yellow counterpane covering his king-sized bed. The silence was oppressive. She lay back with her head on the pillow and stared at the ceiling. Was this the side Rudy slept on, she wondered? Her bed was almost as big. She slept in the middle of hers.

She laid a hand on the bedside table and touched a scented

oil lamp. Was there still oil in it? The room had been shut up for weeks and was stuffy. Some scent would be nice. She sighed. No use delaying any longer. She sat up and opened the drawer, expecting to see a small book with a blue cover, Rudy's diary. The drawer was empty.

———

Dawn had barely tinged the horizon when Oliver was awakened by a pounding on his front door. He leaped out of bed and had his .38 in his hand before he was quite awake enough to realize what was happening. He opened the door to find a familiar cheeky lad in a Western Union uniform standing on the landing. He slipped the .38 behind his back. The boy grinned at his disheveled state and held out a telegram. "You're pretty popular, Mister."

Oliver growled and gave the boy another quarter before shutting the door in his face and ripping open the envelope.

COME SEE ME AS SOON AS YOU CAN *STOP* HAVE
NEW LEADS *STOP* BL

> ~ *Ted Oliver has the feeling*
> *that he is on an out-of-control sled,*
> *Hurtling Downhill* ~

"I guess you found something up at Falcon Lair that you want me to look into," Oliver said.

"My list of suspects has exploded. I don't know where to begin." Bianca had chosen the sunroom for her meeting with Oliver. A sunny, sultry, jungle-like room full of potted plants, this was the first place he had ever seen her in the flesh, and it gave him a peculiar feeling to be here again. She was sitting on the edge of the same chaise lounge with the little dog snuggled up next to her, petting him absently while she talked. She had invited Oliver to sit, but he had laid his hat on the chair and was standing at the open French door, looking out at the gardens while she filled him in.

"Before he died, Rudy told me I should read his diary, that it might give me a clue to who was poisoning him. But the diary wasn't where he said it would be, and I hunted all over the house trying to find it. Before I left, I asked Luther, the groundskeeper, if anyone else had been in the house since Rudy died, and he told me that Pola Negri had spent an entire afternoon at Falcon Lair right before she got on the train to New York. I'll bet any amount of money that she found the diary and took it. I've already telephoned her secretary and made arrangements to meet with her this afternoon. I may not have found the diary, but I found plenty of other papers in Rudy's office. I had no idea how far in debt he actually was. He had written checks for five grand to the man who sold him his Arabian stallion, fifteen grand to the company renovating his house, and almost forty thousand to someone called Tony Cornero..." She hesitated at the expression of surprise on Oliver's face when she said the name.

Oliver recovered quickly. "Whoa! That's a chunk of change, all right."

Bianca was not fooled. "You know who Tony Cornero is."

"Yeah, Tony Cornero—Tony the Hat—is a bootlegger." Was he also blackmailing movie stars? Oliver didn't express the thought to Bianca. "But why was Valentino giving money to Tony? Did you find anything that told what the payments were for?"

"I don't know why he was paying Cornero. I can't imagine Rudy being involved in rum-running. But according to his books, he made several payments of thousands of dollars each to him over the past few months."

"Was Valentino a gambler?"

Her eyes widened and she didn't reply, which Oliver took for a yes.

He said, "Cornero has converted one of his ships, the *Monaco*, into a casino. It's anchored three miles off the coast, west of Long Beach, beyond the reach of U.S. Customs. On the weekends Cornero ferries recreational gamblers out in a fleet of speedboats, and on Thursdays he hosts a special salon just for high rollers. Poker games, baccarat, 21, that sort of thing. I'm sure some of your movie star friends know all about it."

"Rudy certainly never mentioned any such thing to me, but I know he gambled away a lot of money on the tables in Europe over the years. Poor Rudy, he never had a lick of sense." She emitted a frustrated sigh, then straightened. "So, could this have anything to do with Rudy's death?"

"I don't know. Cornero wouldn't want him dead, not if Valentino was dropping as much cash in his casino as you say. But doing business with mobsters isn't healthy. He could have run afoul of some unscrupulous type. Who knows?"

"I know plenty of actors who like to gamble. I'm going to find a way to get myself invited onto the ship and talk to Cornero."

Bianca looked so excited that Oliver was immediately sorry that he had put the notion of the casino into her head. "Now, wait a minute, Bianca. I don't see any reason for you to start snooping around in a gangster's business. That's what you've hired me to do."

She didn't seem to hear him. "Come with me. You can do the snooping while I distract Cornero."

"No, you can't!"

Her eyes narrowed. "What do you mean I can't? I certainly can and I will."

Oliver quelled a feeling of alarm. He was going to have to tell her about Dix. "I'm sorry I didn't tell you before, Bianca, but K. D. Dix wants me to find out how Valentino and Cornero were connected. I don't want her wondering how we know each other."

"Dix?" Bianca repeated the name, just to make sure she hadn't misheard. "Why? Why does she care about Rudy? What is she after?"

Oliver summed up his conversation with Dix for Bianca. "Anyway, she wants me to get onto the *Monaco* and find out who Tony's backers are."

"How is that connected to Rudy's death?"

"I don't think she cares a whit about Valentino. She's looking to take over Cornero's new gambling operation, and my guess is she thinks some other crook is trying to beat her to it, maybe by getting rid of his current backers. She's believes that the Chicago mob wants a foothold here in California and wants to get in on the action before they do. You go talk to Pola Negri, like you planned, find out what she has to say about that diary. I'll make my own arrangements to get onto the *Monaco* and see what I can find out about Tony the Hat."

> *~ Pola Negri,*
> *tragedienne ~*

Pola Negri's house was located just south of Sunset on Beverly Drive, not far from Falcon Lair, or from Bianca's own Orange Garden estate. Funny how we all live in each other's pockets, Bianca thought, as she drove down San Ysidro Canyon to the flats. Bianca had driven past Pola's big white house with its profusion of flowers in the front many times, but she had never been invited inside. Pola gave as many parties as anyone in Hollywood, but she seldom invited single women, unless they were producers or writers or could otherwise do something for her.

Pola's secretary had not been able to hide her skepticism when Bianca telephoned in the morning and asked for a meeting that day. Bianca didn't really expect to be accommodated so quickly, but she had promised Nils Fox that she would report to the studio to finish filming *The Clutching Claw* the next day, and she was desperate to find out if Pola had taken Rudy's diary. She had to try.

She was as surprised as the secretary when Pola invited her to come down that very afternoon.

Pola's sprawling two-story mansion reminded Bianca of an antebellum plantation house, with six white columns standing in an elegant row across the long front porch. Pink oleander bushes in glorious bloom stretched across the entire front of the house and yellow asters lined the curving drive. Several mature date palms scattered across the lawn broke the Deep South illusion, giving the place a distinctly California feel.

A uniformed maid greeted Bianca at the front door and ushered her through the house and out to a deep veranda shaded by a vine-draped trellis. Pola was seated at small round table covered with a white cloth. A silver coffeepot and a china platter of scones were placed enticingly on top, as yet untouched. It was a perfect setting on a perfect sun-drenched day. Pola stood up as Bianca approached. The actress was dressed head to toe in black, her dark hair completely covered with a black scarf. Her face was so pale that Bianca wondered if she was wearing greasepaint. The only color on her person was the bright red of her lips and fingernails. Her large blue-gray eyes were without makeup and seemed sunken. She really does look sad, Bianca thought. She reminded herself that Pola was a very good actress.

Pola waved Bianca toward a chair at the table. She didn't bother with pleasantries. "What do you want, Bianca?"

Bianca had always had some trouble understanding Pola's English. Pola's voice was low-pitched, and she had a heavy Polish accent. In fact, they understood one another better if they spoke French. Pola hadn't been in the United States very long, just since 1923, when director Ernst Lubitsch had brought the well-known European actress to Hollywood. Since Pola hadn't beat around the bush, neither would Bianca. She said, *"Avez-vous volé le journal de Rudy?"*

Pola had not expected to be accused of theft in the space of a minute. "What! You accuse me of taking my darling's journal?"

"Pola, when I saw Rudy for the last time in New York, he told me to retrieve his diary and read it, and he told me exactly where he kept it, in the drawer of his bedside table. Luther told me that you are the only person who has been inside Falcon Lair since Rudy died. He said that he has not even let the maids inside to clean. Yesterday, I was allowed to go in to retrieve the diary, but it is not there. You are the only person who could have moved it. Did you take it? It is important, Pola. We must find that diary."

She had been speaking French, but it might as well have been Swahili to judge by Pola's reaction. "What?" she repeated. "*Porquoi? Porquoi?* Why would he tell *you*? Why would he tell you anything? Why do you care about this journal? My beloved is dead. What difference could it make now, that horrible journal? What difference does anything make now?" Her face had gone from pale to purplish-red and her eyes bulged.

Oh, my God, is she going to have a stroke? Bianca reached for Pola's hand, but she snatched it away. "I don't know how much you have heard about how Rudy died," Bianca said. "Rudy did not want anyone to know, so his manager has kept his secret. Rudy was poisoned. It happened over a long period of time, so he did not know who poisoned him or how. He told me that he wrote everything in his diary, every bad thing anyone said to him, every confrontation, as well as all the good things. That journal may hold the key to who killed him, Pola. Do you have it?"

The sudden rush of color to Pola's face faded as fast as it arose. "*Empoisonné!*" Poisoned. She turned ashen, her eyes rolled back, and she swayed in her chair. Bianca jumped up and grabbed her by both arms. "No fainting! Nobody is buying your act today. Did you take it?"

An expression of terror crossed the actress's face. "But I did not know..."

Bianca couldn't stop herself from giving Pola a good shake. "Pola, what did you do?"

Pola pushed her away. "I found it. It is true. He was dead, so I read it. I read what he said. Then I burned it."

Bianca caught her breath. *Oh, my God,* she thought, *now* I'm *going to have a stroke.* "Why? What was in that book? Do not tell me that you..."

Pola burst into tears, deep, wracking, wet, snotty tears, and covered her face with a serviette. "No, no," she wailed, switching to English. "You do not understand. I could never hurt Rudy. I loved him, truly, truly. But he did not love me. I read the newspapers, the magazines. They say I make a scene at his funeral only for publicity, but it is not true. It is the pain. I say he asked to marry me, because I think what does it matter now? Who will know or care? It was a lie. Yes, I burned the journal. I did not want anyone to know that he loved another. I am sorry. I am sorry."

Between Pola's wailing grief and her Slavic vowels, Bianca could barely make out what she was saying. "I did not read it all, only when I saw my name, or the names of other women. He had many women friends, but only one he loved, and it was not me." Pola reached for a glass of water and guzzled it, dehydrated, before she continued. "His last entry, the day before he left for San Francisco..." Her face crumpled. "...the last day I saw him alive, he wrote that when his debts were paid, he would give up everything for her."

"Who is this love of his, Pola? Did he name her? Was it Natacha?"

Pola looked away. "It does not matter now."

Bianca sank back in her chair as Pola cried. She had been looking at poor Pola Negri the wrong way all along. She had thought Pola's histrionics were for attention, that Pola had been using her connection to the great Valentino to enhance her own fame. But Pola was a victim of that cruelest of ironies. She had fallen in love with someone who didn't love her back. That agony could drive anyone to behave like a fool.

"I'm the one who's sorry, Pola. I'm sorry for my uncharitable thoughts. You really did care for him."

"I adored him."

"I know, hon. Sometimes love is an awful thing." She watched Pola weep, wondering where she was going to go from here. When the tears began to abate, she said, "It's a shame you burned the diary. That's going to make finding Rudy's killer much harder. I don't mean to upset you, but perhaps this woman, this secret love, knows something about Rudy's enemies that we don't. Is her name Jenny?"

Pola looked surprised. "How do you…?"

Shall I tell her that Jenny *is the last word I heard Rudy say before he died?* Unwilling to face another flood, Bianca said, "I overheard him mention the name once. But he never spoke of her to me, or to anyone else, as far as I know."

"Yes, in his journal he called her Jenny, a quiet, gentle girl who wanted nothing from him. He wrote that he would speak to her about the future when he returned from New York."

Bianca could hardly contain herself. At last, a new lead. "What is her last name? Where can I find her?"

"He wrote no last name. He wrote only that he met her a few months ago, while he was working on a picture for Universal or United Artists. I do not remember which, nor do I know exactly when."

"Thank you, Pola. I promise I won't tell anyone what you told me." Let her live in her fantasy and perhaps soothe her broken heart a little by pretending to be Rudy's betrothed. What harm could it do now?

Bianca broke every rule of the road as she sped back up the hill to her estate, eager to telephone Jim Quirk and ask if he knew a Jenny who worked at Universal or maybe UA. The memory of Pola's hysterics in New York still rankled, but her irritation was now tempered with pity. Nothing hurt like unrequited love. Damn, she was beginning to like Pola again.

> ~ *Look who has crawled out of the Woodwork!* ~

On the morning of September 14, 1926, Ted Oliver stood outside the elegant Church of the Good Shepherd on Roxbury

Drive in Beverly Hills, along with hundreds of rubberneckers and press photographers, and watched the elite arrive in their limousines for Valentino's memorial service. The whole she-bang reminded him of a Hollywood premiere. Everyone who was anyone came, dressed in tasteful jewels, furs, feathers, all in fashionable variations of the color black.

He saw Bianca arrive on the arm of her *Dangereuse* co-star, Daniel May. May was a fine-looking young man, much closer to Bianca's tender age than Oliver was. He had light brown hair, dark blue eyes, and a smattering of freckles that gave him an all-American, boyish look. Oliver fought down an irrational stab of jealousy. Bianca's black cloche and drop-waist dress were both outlined with a subtle yellow piping and offset with a yellow neck scarf that added a bit of sunshine to the sad proceedings.

As the pair walked toward the church, Bianca's gaze skewed toward him and an ironic smile appeared before she and May disappeared inside. Oliver banished the thought that she could read his mind.

To his surprise, he did not see a single mobster arrive for the memorial service, at least no one that he knew. If he saw a face that he didn't recognize, he made notes about the person's appearance. Once or twice he asked a man with a camera and a press card tucked in his hatband if he knew who this guy or that guy was. No one more exciting than an assistant director and a scenarist, but he wrote down their names anyway. Oliver stood among the crush of onlookers outside the church for the entire two-hour service, then elbowed his way to his car to fall into the funeral procession as it wound its way from Beverly Hills to Hollywood Memorial Park, where Valentino would be laid to rest for eternity in a borrowed crypt. The screen idol had not made any provision for his own burial. Nobody was prepared to die at thirty-one.

The hired cops tried to toss Oliver out of the procession, of course. His jalopy didn't fit in with all the Rolls-Royces and

Hispano Suizas. But he had a perfectly valid invitation to the crypt-side service, which he swore he hadn't stolen, and George Ullman himself had verified, so they had no choice but to let him bring up the rear. The line of celebrity vehicles was so long that the service was already beginning by the time the last cars were parked in the makeshift lot by the cemetery gate. Oliver had to stand to one side of the rows of white wooden chairs that had been set out for the mourners, but that suited him. He had a much better view of the illustrious crowd. He could see the back of Bianca's head in the front row. She was comforting the veil-draped Pola Negri, whom he could hear weeping even from this distance.

Some of the people who were at the memorial service had not made it to the cemetery, but a few new faces had turned up for the burial. He straightened when he caught sight of Jack Dragna, a mobster just out of prison for extortion, and his right-hand man, Handsome Johnny Roselli. And there, sitting in the middle of the last row, having a friendly conversation with Los Angeles oil magnate Miles Donahue, was Tony the Hat. Oliver pulled his fedora low on his forehead, shading his eyes. So Dix was on the right trail. The Los Angeles mob had an unknown interest in the late, lamented Rudolph Valentino.

~ A Half-Baked Plan is Better Than No Plan At All ~

After the service was over and Valentino properly entombed in a crypt that didn't belong to him, Oliver hung around the cemetery until the last mourner had left. The gangsters didn't linger, and the celebrities and movie folk trickled out at their own pace, some taking the opportunity to talk to agents and producers and make a few deals while they had the opportunity. The last to leave were June Mathis, Mary Pickford, and Bianca LaBelle, supporting a stumbling Pola Negri between them. Bianca surely saw him standing solitary behind the now-empty chairs, but she did not cast him a glance as the women made their way toward the gate.

Oliver left Hollywood Memorial Park and drove directly to Pasadena to talk to Dix. He did not telephone beforehand. He did not stop by his own place to change, even though his shirt was wet with flop sweat. He was afraid that if he hesitated, he'd start thinking, and if he started thinking, he'd decide that his plan might be bold, but it was also dangerous.

He was stopped at the gate of Dix's manse, as he expected, but he managed to talk the guard into notifying Dix that he wanted to see her. He could hear her lilting voice over the intercom speaker. "Certainly. Let him in." She sounded amused.

Dix's goon made him get out of the auto and frisked him so thoroughly that Oliver thought he might as well just go ahead and do a cavity search. Then the pervert wouldn't let him get back behind the wheel.

"You walk," the guy grunted. "I'll park this heap."

So Oliver walked the fifty yards to the front door, where another goon patted him down one more time before letting him step inside.

Dix herself was walking down the hall toward the foyer to meet him. Goon number three, the one Oliver called Juan, glided along behind her.

He scooped off his hat when she halted in front of him. Oliver wasn't the tallest man, but the old woman barely came up to his shoulder. "Well," she said, delighted, "you have shaken loose some new information for me already?"

"I'd like to say that I'm a brilliant investigator, but you're the one who had the right hunch. Guess who I saw among the bereaved at Valentino's burial, looking like the cat who ate the canary?"

"This sounds promising. All right, let's go back to my sitting room."

She led the way and Oliver followed. Juan brought up the rear. Oliver could feel the heat of his malevolence behind him.

Dix settled into her usual armchair and Oliver into his usual spot across the room. Juan took his place next to the potted palm in the corner and faded from existence.

Tea was already on the table, and Dix poured Oliver a cup without asking if he wanted one. He leaned forward to take the pink-flowered cup from her hand before launching into his spiel. "Cornero was at the burial, along with Jack Dragna and his boy Johnny Roselli."

"Indeed! Three bootleggers. Dragna did a stint up the river for blackmail. Maybe he's up to his old tricks."

"They were the only hoods that I recognized. Dragna and Roselli kept to themselves, but Cornero sat at the back during the internment and had a nice conversation with Miles Donahue."

Dix's eyebrows shot up. "Miles Donahue? The oilman?"

"The same. Him and Cornero jawed quite a lot, which surprised me. All I know about Donahue is that he's a big oil magnate and philanthropist and he's rich as Midas. As far as I know, he's an upstanding citizen. I've never heard that he's into anything shady, so why pass the time of day with somebody like Tony the Hat?"

Dix did not look surprised. "Nobody who is rich as Midas is an upstanding citizen, Ted. Donahue is just better at hiding it than some. He and I have never done business, but I know for a fact that he acquired most of his mineral rights through means most unbecoming." She flashed a dimple. "I had heard that he was interested in becoming involved in the entertainment industry. There's a plan afoot by some of the big studios to corner the film distribution market across the country, to make theater owners lease films by the bundle—five dud movies for every blockbuster they want to show. Should be most lucrative. I've invested in it myself. Of course if Donahue's hobnobbing with Tony the Hat, he may be looking to get into liquor smuggling or the offshore casino business. I wonder what this has to do with Valentino? Who else did they talk to? Dragna?"

"I didn't see Cornero talk to anyone else. He left as soon as the ceremony was over. Still, why was Dragna there at all? He had his factotum Roselli with him."

"Oh, these Italians." Dix gave a dismissive wave. "They're all connected in one way or another. Dragna is a heroin smuggler, among other enterprises. Maybe Valentino was a customer."

"Didn't Dragna do time for extortion?"

"He did. That was over ten years ago, though. He tried to get that Black Hand nonsense started out here on the West Coast, but all it got him was three years in the slammer. Since then he's been mostly involved in drugs and gambling."

The Black Hand. Oliver had told Bianca that the Black Hand was old news. Maybe it was. And maybe Jack Dragna was up to his old tricks.

"What about Donahue?" Dix said. "Did he say anything to Dragna?"

"Donahue had a few words with several people, mostly, 'Hi, how are you?' and 'Ain't it a shame about the Sheik?' If he talked to Dragna, I didn't see it. He did spend a few minutes head-to-head with Valentino's manager, George Ullman. The skinny is that Ullman has been named executor of Valentino's estate."

Dix raised an eyebrow. "Not the brother?"

"Apparently not. The brother was there, though."

"What were Donahue and Ullman talking about?"

"Donahue may have been talking to him about the disposition of the estate, trying to get some sort of charitable donation. That would be up his alley. I don't really know. I couldn't get close enough to hear much."

Dix nodded. "Who else was there that I should know about?"

"Like I said, everybody who's anybody was there. If I'd had an autograph book with me, I could have filled it up lickety-split and sold it for a fortune. Ullman and Alberto Valentino and their wives were in the first row, next to the crypt, along with June Mathis and Pola Negri, who sobbed so loud you could hardly hear the padre. Negri fainted a couple of times, too, much to the delight of the photographers. Chaplin was there, and Pickford and Fairbanks, Gloria Swanson and that guy from Massachusetts she's been dating, name of Kennedy, I think. All the broads Valentino did movies with, Bianca LaBelle and Vilma Bánky Alice Terry, and Agnes Ayers. I saw Will Rogers and Sam Warner. Jean Acker, Valentino wife number one, was in the crowd. I stood way off to the side, next to a photographer for the *Beacon*, who pointed out some of Valentino's servants and a couple of his writer and musician friends whose faces I didn't know. I only recognized a couple of the names he said—Louella Parsons and James Quirk. Looking for copy, I expect."

Dix placed her cup on the side table. "Forget about the actors for the moment. I want you to find out if and how Miles Donahue or Jack Dragna are involved with Cornero. Rum running or gambling or something else."

"You think one of them might be trying to horn in on Cornero's business?"

She shrugged. "Maybe."

"And you want to know who your competition is?"

Her dimple reappeared. "Maybe."

"Can you get me on the *Monaco* as soon as possible? Set me up as a fat cat gambler from Seattle with a wad to blow and maybe a yen to invest in the flicks."

"Consider it done," Dix said.

~ We Return to a Farmhouse in China, Where Last we Saw Bianca Dangereuse... ~

...pressing herself against the bricks, listening for a clue to Butch Revelle's whereabouts. The muffled sound of voices draws her to one of the wings of the farmhouse. A dim light comes through a high window—too high for Bianca to peek through. Her brief reconnoiter turns up a wooden bucket, just the thing to serve as a step stool.

Butch is tied to a chair in the middle of the small bare room. She stifles a gasp. He has been badly beaten. The Clutching Claw is standing with his back to her. He is speaking to Butch, though Bianca cannot hear him well enough to understand what he is saying. Not that it matters.

She steps off the bucket and picks it up by the handle, giving it a couple of swings to test its weight. It is a sturdy bucket. Solid oak. It will make quite a dent in the Clutching Claw's skull. She steps to the door, tensed to make her move, and smashes the tyrant over the head.

He slides soundlessly to the ground. Butch gasps and emits a low moan, but Bianca puts a finger to her lips. Do not alert the guards. She withdraws her knife from the sheath on her belt and quickly cuts Butch's bonds.

His injuries are so severe he cannot stand. Bianca positions herself under his arm and lifts him from the chair. She guides him toward the door. He is bravely doing his best, but he is dragging one leg behind him, useless. Her heart falls. She cannot make a stealthy escape with Butch in this condition. She is going to have to eliminate the guards. Somehow.

She gently returns her wounded cousin to his chair and draws her Luger.

———

"All right, cut! Well done," director Nils Fox said. "Let's break for lunch and meet back here at one."

One of the Chinese perimeter guards spoke up. "Do we need to rehearse the fight scene where Wu and I try to stop her escape?" He nodded toward his fellow bit actor.

"I think that's a good idea," Bianca said, relishing the idea of tossing the two very large stuntmen about. The stunt people were always a lot of fun to work (play) with.

"Let's finish shooting the rescue scene first, then the four of you can go over the fight choreography before we resume shooting after lunch."

The Clutching Claw had been put on hold due to Rudy's death, but time was a-wasting and so was money. Bianca was eager to pursue her investigation, but she couldn't help but feel relieved to get back to work. Weeks of fear and worry and grief had exhausted her and made it difficult for her to think clearly. Perhaps a few days of movie action and adventure would clear her mind.

After lunch and before shooting resumed, the actors returned to the makeup chair for a touch-up. It was wonderful to lie back, close your eyes, and leave the job to a professional. When Bianca had first started in motion pictures, a mere five years earlier, she had done her own makeup, obliterating her features with white greasepaint, lining her eyes with kohl and darkening her lids and lips with purple eyeshadow and lipstick. She had even whitened her hands with chalk to match the ghostly hue of her face. Fortunately, the quality of film had improved so much in the past couple of years that she could now sport a more natural look on the screen.

The woman doing her makeup on this movie was a middle-aged native Californio woman with the unlikely name of Thelma Sanchez McAndrew, who considered herself as much therapist as aesthetician.

Thelma wrapped a towel around Bianca's neck and critically eyed her reflection in the mirror. "You look terrible, darling."

"Thanks ever so much, Thelma."

"Well, it's no wonder. It was a dreadful thing about Mr. Valentino." She began dabbing lightener under Bianca's eyes. "Is it true that he was murdered?"

Bianca's eyes snapped open. "Where did you hear that?"

"I read it in the *Hollywood Globe*, dear. They said that he was really shot to death by a jealous husband and the whole perforated ulcer story was just a ruse."

Bianca felt her shoulders relax. "I guarantee that isn't true. I spent quite a lot of time with him in the hospital before he died and there were no bullets involved."

Thelma squeezed a measure of foundation into her palm and smoothed it over Bianca's already smooth cheeks. "I'm so glad to hear that. Mr. Valentino never struck me as someone who would be mixed up with a married woman, in spite of all the gossip. I figured that if anyone knew the truth, it would be you. I'm sorry. I know you two were friendly. He was always such a sweetheart."

"Thank you. He was."

"Still, darling, you should try to get more sleep. These dark circles under your eyes look tragic."

"I promise I'll do better, Thelma." Bianca removed the towel from her neck and stood. "Even though you are a magician. I do look much better." She was distracted by the reflection of the assistant director waving at her in the mirror, trying to catch her attention.

"Miss LaBelle," said the AD, "James Quirk is on the telephone for you."

———

"Jimmy, what did you find out?"

"You gave me an impossible task, Bianca. There must be fifty Jennys who work in the business, and there's no guarantee that Rudy's Jenny is one of them. Maybe she was a waitress who was nice to him once. It was like trying to find a needle in a haystack."

The tone of his voice as he complained was too triumphant to fool Bianca. "But you found her!"

"Hang on. Maybe or maybe not. I cross-referenced all the names you gave me to search for with the studios where Rudy worked and came up with one girl that seems to fit all your criteria. She started working as a personal assistant for George Fitzmaurice when he was directing *The Son of the Sheik* at United Artists, but she quit a few weeks ago. Her name is Jenny Donahue."

"Donahue! Any relation to Miles Donahue, the oil millionaire?"

"I don't know and neither did her replacement at the studio. Donahue isn't the most common Irish name, but it isn't the rarest, either. The new secretary didn't know where Jenny went after she quit. Fitzmaurice wasn't in when I called, so I didn't talk to him. He might know."

"Jimmy, you are a pearl among men. I didn't think it could be done, but you did it."

Quirk chuckled. "I was afraid that if I didn't, you'd wake me up at four in the morning again and harass me, like you did today."

"I'm sorry, but I had to be on set at five and I wanted to get the ball rolling."

"You owe me an exclusive interview now, you know."

"Jimmy, I do owe you. Oops, Nils is giving me a dirty look. I have to go. I'm going to go see Fitzmaurice as soon as I can. I'll let you know if I find Jenny." She hung up the phone, elated. Jenny Donahue was Rudy's Jenny, she was sure of it. She had seen Miles Donahue at the funeral. She had seen him talking to Tony Cornero. It could not all be a coincidence.

She stalked back to the set, impatient and hungry to get on with her investigation and grill the director George Fitzmaurice. Perhaps pounding on two enormous Chinese stuntmen would be good therapy.

> ~ *Later that Afternoon, Bianca takes a meeting*
> *With George Fitzmaurice* ~

Bianca knew director, producer, and all-around artist George Fitzmaurice fairly well. He had directed her in a light comedy a couple of years earlier and they still had an occasional luncheon together. Fitzmaurice was born in Paris, and though he had been in the States for decades, he still enjoyed conversing with Bianca in French over a glass of wine. Fitz, as she knew him, had also directed Rudy in *The Son of the Sheik*, the movie Rudy was promoting in New York when he died.

He was in the midst of directing a drama with Vilma Banky and Ronald Colman and had invited her to meet him at the office United Artists had provided for him on the lot. It was a creaky little room but close to the studio where he was shooting. He invited Bianca to have a seat on the one chair in the office that didn't sag, lean, or have lumps. Fitz opted to lean against his desk and offered her a cup of coffee.

She waved the offer away. "Fitz, I'm trying to find someone, and I'm hoping you can help me."

"Certainly, Bianca. I'll do anything I can for you. Of course I'd like for you to do something for me, too."

Bianca stiffened, wary. Her fame gave her power and a certain amount of protection, but she was still a young woman in Hollywood who had fended off plenty of filthy propositions from producers, directors, other actors, and members of the general public who thought they were in love with her.

Fitzmaurice continued, unaware of her discomfort. "I've acquired the rights to Wickfield's latest bestseller *The Death of Lucretia,* and Universal is going to produce it. You'd be perfect as the woman who brings down the last king of Rome with her suicide."

Bianca let out a breath that she didn't know she was holding. "Send me the script and I'll have a look at it. Of course you'll have to get UA's permission for me to do a picture for Universal, but I don't think that'll be a problem. Do you have the financing in place?"

"Almost. I hope to start shooting early next year."

"I'm committed to this *Grand Obsession* tour early next year. Now that Rudy is gone, they'll never let me shorten it. Still interested?"

"Hell, yes. We will push back the shoot if we can get Bianca LaBelle. I'll arrange for a courier to hand-deliver a copy of the treatment to your house as soon as it is done."

"On second thought, send it to my agent. He'll forward it to me if he thinks it's a fit. Now, Fitz, I hear that your previous secretary was a woman named Jenny."

Fitzmaurice blinked. "Yes, Jenny Donahue."

"Was she friends with Rudy, do you know?"

"I don't know. I know they met. He came to my office several times while she worked here, but I can't tell you if there was more to it than that. What's this about?"

Bianca felt her heart rate pick up. "Do you know if she's any relation to Miles Donahue, the oil millionaire?"

"His daughter. But don't mention it to her. She hates the guy."

"Why? I thought Donahue was big into charity and good works."

"I don't know. She never told me. I thought it was odd that they don't get along, though. She is a lovely girl, and her father seemed like a nice enough fellow the one time I met him."

Oh, my God, what a tangle. Rudy's mysterious Jenny was the daughter of Miles Donahue, whom Bianca had seen talking to the mobster Tony Cornero at Rudy's funeral. The same Tony Cornero to whom Rudy had paid thousands of dollars for an unknown reason. Tony Cornero, who owned a gambling ship called the *Monaco*—the same ship that Oliver told her about. Did all these unlikely links create a chain that could lead Bianca to Rudy's killer? She staved off a stab of uncertainty and soldiered on. "Do you know where she is now? I want to find her and talk to her, if I can."

"I don't know, I'm sorry. She didn't leave a forwarding address. I got the feeling that she didn't want to be found. I tried to talk her out of leaving. She was the best secretary I ever had. Very efficient."

> *~ It's easy to be bold
> in the daylight ~*

The guard at the gate to Bianca's estate knew Oliver by now and waved him through with only a cursory sneer. Oliver parked his Ford in the drive and pounded on the door, then lit a cigarette to pass the time while whoever was inside could make the long trek across the foyer.

He had only taken a single drag when the giant entryway

swung open and Fee appeared. The majordomo was clad in a silk dressing gown and a terrycloth head wrap. Fee was never without some sort of head covering. Oliver supposed there was hair under there, but he had never seen it. Fee gestured for Oliver to step into the foyer, where they eyed one another for a silent moment.

Oliver took the initiative and said, "I know she wasn't expecting me, but I've some news."

"You should have called," Fee said. "She isn't here. She's gone to dinner at the Fairbankses' house. She goes there every Tuesday evening. You'd have saved yourself a trip if you'd called first."

Oliver didn't bother to defend his action. Fee knew perfectly well that Oliver never called first, not from his flat, at least. Maybe his phone was tapped and maybe it wasn't, but he never took the chance. "When will she be back?"

"She usually returns very late. I can relay a message."

"I'd rather tell her in person."

Fee did not appear to be affronted. "As you wish. If it's important for you to talk to her tonight, you can wait for her in the sunroom. It might be a long wait."

Oliver thought about it. Jack Dempsey had followed Fee into the entryway and was currently sniffing around his feet and giving him the stink eye. Oliver tried not to laugh. He admired the ratty little canine. The mutt might have been the size of a chipmunk, but he thought he was a lion. Oliver would have tried to pet him, but he was afraid he'd lose a finger.

He looked up at Fee, who was waiting patiently for an answer. He wondered if Fee slept on the floor across the door to Bianca's bedroom, like a harem guard. "On second thought," Oliver said, "you can relay a message for me. Tell her that Dix has arranged for me to go out to the *Monaco* on Thursday night. I'll come by on Friday to tell her what I find out. She will be receiving on Friday morning, will she not?"

"She will be on set Friday morning. Come back after eight o'clock on Friday night."

Oliver raised an eyebrow. "The great LaBelle won't be at a party on Friday night?"

Fee scooped the pup off the floor and tucked him under an arm. "Not since Mr. Valentino died."

That set Oliver back a little. "Oh, well, tell her that if she needs to get hold of me before then, she can send me a telegram like she's been doing, or try me at Bay Cities Italian Deli in Santa Monica. Hey, Fee, I hope she hasn't come up with any more harebrained schemes. You tell her that she ought to stick with her movie pals and leave the mobsters to me, like we planned."

Fee didn't reply. Oliver took another drag of his Lucky Strike. Fee hadn't asked his opinion about Bianca's investigation, but he needed to express one to somebody and Fee was handy.

"What a broad!" Oliver said on a smoky exhalation. "She thinks she can do anything, and as far as I've been able to see, nobody has proved her wrong. Yet. It's unnatural for such a young woman to be so..."

"So what?" Fee's tone indicated no small amount of umbrage at Oliver's comment.

"I don't know. Independent. Self-sufficient. Most babes are looking for a little romance or companionship, or they think they can fix you, or they want somebody to take care of them..."

Fee made a disparaging noise. "You're a prick, Oliver. Like most guys."

Oliver gave Fee a narrow look. It dawned on him that he was actually growing used to the appearance of this colossal person of unspecified sex. "Hey, what's your story, Fee?"

The question was unexpected, but Fee was not surprised. The dog wiggled and made a noise of protest. Fee put him on the floor. "Wouldn't you like to know?"

"Oh, come on. We're friends, aren't we? I'm not going to tell anybody anything."

"No, you're not, because you'll never know anything to tell."

Oliver was amused. "How long have you worked for Bianca?"

Fee hesitated before deciding that the question was harmless enough. "About four years. I was working for Miss Bolding when I first met her, but Bianca asked me to set up her household after she got famous, and I just stayed on."

"How is Alma these days? Last I heard she got tossed off the set of her latest flick for always showing up half in the bag."

"Not that it's any of your business, but she's doing much better. Bianca arranged for her to have a nice rest at a spa near Calistoga."

"So the child becomes the parent, eh?"

"Something like that."

"Listen, Fee, I like Bianca a lot, and I worry about her. She's headstrong as hell, and too young to have much sense, I think. As talented and..." He hesitated, searching for the right word. "...competent as she seems to be, I'm afraid she's going to get herself into a situation that she can't get out of and really get hurt."

Fee's skeptical expression softened the tiniest bit. "That's what I'm here for, Oliver, to take care of her." Fee leaned forward and slipped a cigarette out of the ivory box on the telephone table, taking a moment to light it and draw in a leisurely lungful of smoke before continuing. "Besides, Bianca isn't as heedless as she seems. The girl is a thinker." A column of smoke drifted toward the ceiling. "More than once, I've caught her wandering around the house in her pajamas or curled up on the living room couch in the middle of the night..."

Oliver could believe that. "Plotting."

"...brooding. Bianca's already been hurt, Oliver. She's already lost more than you know or are ever likely to."

"Well, now you've really made me curious."

"I'm just explaining a thing or two. It's true she's young. She likes excitement too much. But don't underestimate Bianca. There's more to her than meets the eye." Fee crushed the cigarette butt in a crystal ashtray before opening the front door and, with a sweeping gesture, ushering Oliver out.

> *~ While Oliver talks to Fee,*
> *Bianca has dinner with Movie Royalty ~*

Mary Pickford and Douglas Fairbanks were the reason Bianca had built her house in the wealthy San Ysidro Canyon enclave above Beverly Hills. Bianca's Orange Garden estate was a wonder to behold, but just up the hill, Doug and Mary's Pickfair mansion put her house to shame. Bianca grew up with nine siblings in a two-bedroom farmhouse and had not yet learned the art of profligacy. Mary was doing her best to teach her. It was Mary who had educated Bianca about art in all its forms, and she didn't have to travel far to provide exquisite examples to her student. Pickfair was practically a museum, filled with stunning pieces of Chinese ceramics and *objets,* Remington paintings and sculptures, eighteenth-century French furniture. The house itself, a twenty-five room, four-story mock-Tudor mansion, was a knockout, with parquet floors, mahogany paneling, gold leaf trim on the walls, and frescoed ceilings. The Fairbankses had their own screening room and a bowling alley in the basement. Their impressive in-ground swimming pool, a relatively new development for private homes, had inspired Bianca to build her own.

Mary Pickford was "America's Sweetheart," with her wide, blue eyes and golden curls, an actress beloved by the public as well as her peers. But Mary was anything but innocent. Sharp and capable, one of the original founders of United Artists Studios, she had business sense to spare. She had helped Bianca learn to invest and manage her newly gained riches. Doug, on the other hand, was as flamboyant as his swashbuckling movie persona. He was eccentric and charming and a bit of a rogue, but he was good hearted and seemed devoted to Mary, which put him firmly in Bianca's good graces.

The guest list for the regular Tuesday night dinner for the Fairbankses' close friends varied in size and composition, depending on who was available. They were often joined by their nearest neighbors, Charlie Chaplin and his child bride, Leta Grey, but on this evening Charlie was dealing with a disastrous fire at his studio and Leta was at home taking care of two infant sons and stewing with resentment for her spectacularly unfaithful husband.

Tonight it was just Doug, Mary, and Bianca at dinner, so they forewent the dining room and the three of them enjoyed an informal meal of barbecued ribs and beer around a table in Doug's reconstructed Old West–style saloon with its polished mahogany bar backed by a gilded mirror.

Bianca had often expressed her particular delight at Doug's whimsical saloon, which was why Mary had suggested it tonight. She had a motherly attitude toward Bianca, whom she had met at Alma Bolding's house back in 1920, when Bianca was a green fifteen-year-old. Alma had been responsible for bringing young Blanche Tucker to California and had been a wonderful guardian and mentor to the girl at first. Now that Alma had gone off the rails with her drugs and boozing, Bianca found herself turning often to Mary for advice and help, and Mary was only too happy to oblige.

Bianca did her best to be a good guest and engaging conversationalist, but Mary saw through her before dessert was served.

"What's troubling you tonight, darling? Are you still sad about Rudy?"

Bianca put down her corn on the cob and sagged back into her seat with a sigh. "I suppose I am. His death hit me hard, I guess. But I don't want to end such a lovely dinner on a sad note. It's nice to talk about something pleasant for a change."

But Mary's gaze sharpened as she looked at Bianca, taking stock. Even the ebullient Doug suddenly looked serious. He said, "Missy, my girl, I had a chat with George Fitzmaurice yesterday."

"It might do you good to talk about it, darling," Mary said. "Maybe we can help you."

Bianca's heart sank. So much for keeping her murder investigation a secret. She had sworn Pola Negri to silence after she told her that Rudy had been poisoned, but this was Hollywood. Everybody in town was going to be speculating about Valentino's death now.

She rubbed her eyes, suddenly tired and uncertain. Maybe they could help her. If nothing else, maybe they could convince her that she was on a fool's errand. She dropped her hands into her lap and opened her eyes.

Mary was gazing at her expectantly. Doug looked like he was going to leap over the table and do something heroic. Bianca took a deep breath and told them the whole story.

When she was done, Mary reached across the tabletop and took her hand. "Oh, darling, there has been a lot of gossip about Rudy's death, but I thought that was all it was, gossip. If you hadn't told me that the doctor confirmed that he was poisoned, I'd have never believed it. What can we do?"

"I don't know. Help me make sense of all this. I saw Rudy's checkbook. He wrote forty thousand dollars' worth of checks to Tony Cornero. How could Rudy let himself get involved with a bootlegger? Rudy doesn't...didn't even drink that much."

But Doug was not surprised. "Well, Rudy liked to gamble, even though he wasn't very good at it. He was one of the regulars at the Thursday night high-stakes poker game at Casa del Mar," he said, naming an exclusive private club on Santa Monica Beach, within sight of the pier, "and he usually dropped a bundle. Cornero supplies the booze to the club at Casa del Mar and would occasionally sit in on the game. That's probably how Rudy met him. Cornero's a good-natured guy, for a mobster. I know Tony has been interested in getting into offshore gambling for ages. Rudy probably invested in Tony's gambling ship idea. The *Monaco* has turned out to be quite the moneymaker. It's a shame Rudy didn't live to see a return on his investment. He could have paid off all his debts with the proceeds and had plenty to spare."

"There's a regular poker game at the club?" Bianca was surprised. She had recently joined the Casa del Mar beach club herself. "Isn't gambling illegal in California?"

"So's hootch, Missy. The police ignore what goes on at the club. The mayor of Los Angeles and the Santa Monica police chief are members. I sit in on the game a couple times a month. Mary doesn't approve, but I manage to win about as much as I lose. But we don't meet at the club anymore, not since Tony set us up in one of the private salons on the *Monaco*."

"Do you know who else invested in the *Monaco*?"

"I don't know for sure. I'd have to guess. Cornero pitched the scheme at the club a couple of times, so I expect some of the regulars got in on the action."

"I hope you're not one of them, Douglas!" Mary had not offered an opinion on her husband's less-than-legal activities until now.

"Of course not, sweetheart." Doug waited until Mary turned to reach for the ribs before he gave Bianca an exaggerated guilty look.

Mary returned the platter to the center of the table. "I don't see how any of this has to do with someone poisoning Rudy."

"I don't know either," Bianca admitted. "But it's all too interconnected to not to mean something. Who are the regulars at your game, Doug?"

"Mostly actors and businessmen. Chaplin, of course. Buster Keaton and Barrymore—John, not Lionel—are usually there. Harry Chandler and Miles Donahue never miss a game." There were others on his list, but Bianca had heard the name that interested her most and interrupted his recitation.

"Miles Donahue? Can you introduce me to Donahue?"

Doug cast a questioning glance at his wife. "I don't really know the man. I've never seen him anywhere but at the poker game. All I know about him is that he has money to blow and he's not a good loser."

"But you say he never misses a game and the games are always on the *Monaco*?"

"Yes to both. What are you thinking, young lady?"

"Do women ever play in your poker game?"

"Sure, sometimes, if they've got the dough. Gloria Swanson cleaned us all out a few months ago."

Mary was alarmed at the direction the conversation was taking. "Oh, now, Bianca..."

"I was going out to that ship anyway, but now I'm determined to get into the game, Mary. I've got to talk to Miles Donahue."

Mary knew Bianca well enough to see that argument would be futile. "Well, you're not going without Doug to protect you."

"Now, wait a minute." Doug was looking befuddled by the turn in the conversation.

As far as Bianca was concerned, the matter had been decided. "I hear you have to be invited. Who do I talk to to get an invitation?"

Doug surrendered to the inevitable with his usual good humor. "I'll get you one. You're Bianca LaBelle. I don't think you'll have any problem."

~ Ted Oliver Prepares to Spend an Evening
on the High Seas, Rubbing Shoulders with the Elite ~

Oliver expected he would have to take the train from Santa Monica to Long Beach, but Dix sent a car for him. He supposed that a car and driver suited his wealthy gambler persona better than did public transportation. Besides, he would have looked funny riding the milk train in a tuxedo. The touring car that pulled up in front of his building wasn't a limousine, but it was still worth more than everything Oliver owned.

Oliver slid into the back seat and sank into the Moroccan leather upholstery. As the car pulled away from the curb, he patted the wad of bills in his inside breast pocket and adjusted his cuffs before he recognized the driver by the back of his block-like head. "Juan! What are you doing here? Who's watching Her Nibs?"

In the rearview mirror, he could see two bushy eyebrows

draw together in annoyance. "I'm going with you," Juan said. "I'm listed on the invitation as your valet. Mrs. Dix wants to protect her investment." Oliver had never heard Juan speak before. His voice suited his physique, hard and gruff and scary.

"How nice of her. But I work alone. You'll just draw attention that I don't need."

The bodyguard grunted his lack of interest in Oliver's opinion, which made Oliver chuckle. He could just as well have expressed his concern to a rock for all the effect it had. But he really didn't mind the big man's presence. A "manservant" would lend credence to his disguise as Seattle lumber magnate Oliver Nash (his mother's maiden name), and he knew from experience that Juan knew how to be invisible.

Juan drove south along the coast highway, a spectacular, sometimes heart-stopping trip along beaches and little pastel towns and cliffside roads that dropped into the ocean, scenery that calmed Oliver's nerves in spite of himself. It was dark by the time they pulled off the road onto a deserted stretch of sand south of Long Beach. A few yards from the highway, near the black slash of ocean, Oliver could see the dark figures of a dozen or so people milling around, laughing and talking. It sounded like a party.

As he neared the group, he was approached by a tuxedoed young man with a thin build, thin lips, and thin hair who demanded to see "Mr. Nash's" invitation. After inspecting it carefully, the thin man pointed at the hulking figure standing behind Oliver, a wordless question.

Oliver said, "This is my man, Juan."

The thin man nodded. "My name is Elias, and I'll be your escort tonight, Mr. Nash. Come with me and I'll introduce you to the other guests. Only one water taxi is running to and from the *Monaco* tonight, every hour on the hour. The first run from shore to ship will be in about half an hour, so in the meantime, please enjoy the company and a complimentary cocktail. Your man can have a beer with the other servants, just over there."

Elias led Oliver to the group on the beach, where he was handed a martini and left to mingle. Without a word, Juan joined the hoi polloi in their little lower-class ghetto down the beach.

Before he had been drafted into Dix's service, Oliver had done quite a bit of investigative work for the wealthy around the Los Angeles area, so he knew the possibility existed that he would be recognized, especially if any of the gamblers had been involved in a nasty divorce or a homosexual affair. But Oliver was counting on the fact that even if someone did find his face familiar, they'd never connect the pomaded dandy of this evening with his usual rumpled self.

Yet the first thing anyone said to him was, "Say, didn't I see you at Valentino's funeral?"

The sun was long down, so the beach party was lit by torches stuck into the sand. Oliver peered at the tall middle-aged man, trying to put a name to the face. His heart leaped when he recognized James Quirk. "I just got into town from Seattle yesterday," Oliver said, dodging the question. "Nash is the name and lumber is the game. I'm in Los Angeles to do some business, but I figured that a night of good booze, good company, and gorgeous dames would do me good."

"Quite right, Mr. Nash!" The man held out a hand and Oliver shook it. A firm grip and an honest, direct gaze. "James Quirk of *Photoplay* magazine. This is my fiancée, May." He put an arm around an attractive blond woman in a white gown and white fox stole whom Oliver recognized immediately.

"May Allison." He grasped her hand with a little bow. "I saw you in *Flapper Wives*."

She emitted a tinkling laugh. "Fancy you remembering that. That was a while back."

"You made a big impression on me, Miss Allison. And speaking of Valentino's funeral, Mr. Quirk, I believe you interviewed him for your magazine, didn't you?"

Quirk's face fell. "Yes, while he was shooting his last picture,

Grand Obsession, with Bianca LaBelle. That issue hasn't been released yet. I also interviewed him for *The Son of the Sheik*. That particular interview had just gone to print when he died. A terrible loss."

"Ah, yes. Well, I guess that's why you have the funeral on your mind. I read about it in the paper. Sounds like everybody who's anybody in Hollywood showed up."

"That is the truth. In fact, some of the people who were at the Hollywood funeral service are here tonight. I suppose everyone is eager for some distraction after such a sad week."

"I'm just a poor little rich boy from Washington state, so I'm feeling pretty starstruck here amongst all the famous faces. What would you say to introducing me around a bit before we hit the casino and I win all these people's money?"

Fortunately, Quirk thought Oliver's sass was funny. "Certainly," he said.

Oliver followed the writer and May Allison to a group of beautifully dressed drunks who were gathered around a torchlit teakwood bar on the sand, loudly talking about the latest studio contract outrage. Quirk first introduced him to someone very famous. Oliver never remembered who it was, because he only had eyes for a tall, elegant brunette in a slinky red and gold evening gown covered with sequins that sparkled like stars in the torchlight. As she moved, Oliver couldn't keep his eyes off of the slit in the skirt of her gown that bared one long leg from ankle to above her shapely knee.

"Bianca LaBelle," he said, interrupting his introduction to Very Famous Person. He may have insulted someone who was not used to being ignored by walking away from him as though he didn't exist, but Oliver didn't care. He expected that neither Quirk nor Very Famous Person were all that surprised at his rudeness, either. When Bianca LaBelle was present, this sort of thing probably happened a lot.

He wanted to shake her. He wanted to hiss, "What the hell

do you think you're doing?" He wanted to hustle her out of here *tout de suite.* He could do none of these things without making a fuss and blowing his cover.

"Miss LaBelle," he said. "I'm Oliver Nash. I'm a fan." Bianca gave him an insouciant grin over her highball glass and shook his proffered hand.

"It's always nice to meet a fan," she said, and gestured to her right. "This is Douglas Fairbanks."

Oliver hadn't noticed the sleek gentleman with the mustache who was standing next to Bianca. Fairbanks—actor, director, producer, and swashbuckler extraordinaire—hardly needed an introduction. He and his wife, Mary Pickford, had also been Bianca's mentors and protectors since she was a teen, when she first ventured into the jungle that was Hollywood.

Fairbanks favored him with his signature jaunty grin. "Good evening, Mr. Nash. What brings you out among the decadent hordes tonight?"

Oliver repeated his Seattle lumber baron story while sizing up the star. Fairbanks was a trim, compact man, shorter than Oliver would have expected. In fact, he was about the same height as Bianca, who was a tall woman.

When the introductions were done, a man beside the bar caught Fairbanks's attention and he excused himself to wander off and discuss business. Oliver sidled up to Bianca to scold her while he had the chance.

"How is it that Mary Pickford lets her husband squire you out for an evening of gambling and general debauchery?" He kept his voice low to thwart eavesdroppers.

"It was Mary's idea. She thinks he can keep me out of trouble. Besides, Doug still thinks of me as a little girl. As far as he's concerned, he's babysitting tonight. By the way, he knows who you are. I told him everything."

Oliver felt marginally better when he heard that, but he wasn't going to let her know it. "And I told you not to get involved with these rumrunner mugs. I can take care of this investigation perfectly well without your help, and I don't need to be worrying about you while I'm dealing with a gaggle of criminals."

Her nostrils flared. She did not take well to being reproached, as well he knew. He couldn't help himself.

"I have no intention of 'getting involved' with Cornero or his cronies." Her icy tone chilled him. "I'm paying you good money to do that for me. I'm on another errand altogether. I'm looking for a girl, someone who knew Rudy and may be able to fill in some blanks about the last few months of his life. I heard her father will be on the *Monaco* tonight. Doug knows him and has agreed to introduce me. So, mind your own business, Mr. Nash, and I'll mind mine."

Before Oliver was able to continue his argument, Juan appeared. "The motorboats are coming, boss. Let's go."

Oliver offered Bianca his arm. "May I escort you, Miss LaBelle?"

She was still miffed. "No, thank you, Mr. Nash. I have my own escort tonight."

Bianca walked away from Oliver without a backward glance, her spangled dress flashing in the torchlight. He spat out a couple of words he had not used since he was in the army, then followed Juan to the floating pier to board the water taxi.

> ~ The Monaco ~
> ~ Glitz, Glitter, and Sin on the High Seas ~

The taxi comfortably seated forty people in its covered cabin, and another ten or fifteen could be accommodated on deck. It was a star-filled, cool, calm night, so the fifteen-minute trip across the three miles of frighteningly black ocean expanse was smooth. The two-hundred-eighty-foot converted cargo ship *Monaco* loomed up out of the darkness, looking for all the world like a sea monster that had arisen from the ocean depths. As they grew closer,

Oliver was comforted to see that the main deck was lined with lifeboats. Oliver counted three decks above the waterline, and thought the ship bore a slight resemblance to Noah's ark. The ferry cut its engine and maneuvered up to the gangway steps to discharge its passengers.

Much of the promenade deck had been converted into one large open casino. Oliver had learned that Cornero had done his best to recreate a replica of the Casino in Monte Carlo. Since Oliver had never been to Monte Carlo, he wouldn't know the difference, but he had to admit that Cornero's main casino was impressive. It stretched nearly the length of the ship and was beautifully decorated in a mock Belle Epoque style, with blue and gold furniture and walls, a shell-motif skylight, faux marble Corinthian columns, and a huge crystal chandelier. Roulette wheels, blackjack tables, craps, baccarat, slots, any game a risk-taker could desire was available. An usher was posted at the head of a red-carpeted marble staircase that led down to a lower deck, where the private gaming rooms were located. Since Thursday nights were reserved for invitation-only high-stakes gaming, most of the gamblers who had come out on Oliver's ferry headed directly for the stairs.

Oliver's plan tonight was simply to make himself known to Cornero as a wealthy visitor from Washington. He didn't expect to find out much about Cornero's business arrangements in one night, so he had talked Dix into letting him spend her money in the casino for three or four Thursday nights in a row, if necessary. Oliver was not a bad gambler for an amateur and hoped to come out on the winning side. In fact, if he could win big, that would draw Cornero's attention and perhaps earn him an introduction. As a bonus, Dix had told him that he could keep any money he won above the stake she had provided him. As the glittering crowd trooped across the polished oak floors toward the stairs, they passed a mahogany counter for changing out chips with a gilded sign on the side that read *Bank*. Underneath the sign, a flyer announced that the Bank was also a currency exchange for

Mexican and Canadian visitors. Cornero's bootlegging business must be doing very well, or his backers were very rich, for him to be able to afford all this.

With Juan behind him, Oliver descended the staircase to the lower deck to find that they had stepped into an elegant restaurant with a long buffet. Doors off the restaurant space led into the private salons, each with a sign naming the game and the minimum buy-in to join.

"Impressive," Oliver said to the usher. "What's on the deck below?"

"That's a private area, sir. The kitchen, crew quarters, offices. May I answer any question you have about the salons, sir?"

Oliver's best game was poker, though he usually did all right at 21. "Is there a Texas Hold'em game going on anywhere tonight?"

"There is, sir, in the *Salle Blanche*. The ante is five hundred dollars. I'd be glad to see if there is an open seat at the table tonight."

The White Room. "*Salle Blanche*! Sounds lucky to me. Yes, if a seat is available, I'd like to sit in on that game, thank you."

The usher trotted off, leaving Oliver and Juan in the restaurant, where a waiter trotted up and offered them both drinks. Oliver slid his hand into the pocket of his trousers and fingered the roll of bills Dix had given him, wondering who the other high rollers in the salon would be. Was he going to rub shoulders with the stars? Where did Bianca end up? He had lost sight of her and Fairbanks after they disembarked the ferry.

"What do you want me to do while you're blowing Dix's money?" Juan said, jolting Oliver out of his reverie.

It hadn't occurred to Oliver that his "servant" probably wouldn't be allowed into the private salon with him. "I don't know, Juan. Let's see if I'm going to be able to get in on this game first."

The usher returned before Juan had a chance to respond. "I'm sorry, sir, but all the seats at the tables are taken until at least eleven, when one of the regular players has indicated he must leave. If you'd like, I will see that the open seat is held for you, and if another player drops out before that, I'd be glad to notify you."

Oliver slipped a five-dollar bill into the usher's hand. "I'd be grateful."

The fin disappeared into the usher's pocket. "In the meantime, is there another game you'd like to try?"

Oliver considered for a moment. "Perhaps I'll go back upstairs and try my hand at the roulette table for an hour or so, then come back down for a late supper while I wait for the seat to open up. Will the restaurant be open all night?"

"Certainly, sir. An excellent plan. I will look for you in the restaurant at eleven."

The usher's attention was caught by another passenger frantically waving from the passageway, and he scurried away.

Oliver beckoned for Juan to follow him as he headed for the stairs. Instead of going up to the promenade deck, he stepped over the chain that blocked off the stairwell and went down.

"Let's have a look around down here while we have the chance, Juan," he said over his shoulder.

Oliver could feel the big man's breath on the back of his neck as he snarled, "Quit calling me Juan."

"What, you don't like Juan?"

"That ain't my name."

They had reached the lower deck, and Oliver paused to get his bearings. "If it ain't Juan, what is it?"

"None of your business."

Oliver began walking down the passageway, examining the doors. "I've got to call you something."

"Call me 'hey, you.'"

"You don't have a name?"

"Not as far as you're concerned."

Oliver was enjoying this exchange more than he ought. "Well, it's going to look peculiar to all these highfalutin types if I don't know my valet's name."

The big man huffed in annoyance. "Well, shit. You might as well call me Juan, then."

Oliver tried not to laugh. There were some wits under all that muscle. "Okay, then," he said, all business again. "You check the doors on that side of the deck, I'll check these. Holler if you find an empty office."

"What do I tell any mugs I run across?"

"Act drunk and head for the stairs. Tell them you're looking for the men's room. It probably happens all the time."

"Ladder," Juan said.

"What?"

"Stairs are called a ladder on a ship. The floor's the deck and the walls are bulkheads."

"Who the hell cares? What, were you in the Navy or something?"

"I was, during the war."

"Well, let's just speak English tonight, shall we?" Oliver had just moved past a room with a sign on it that said *Purser*. "We can exchange biographies when and if we get out of this in one piece. Shut up and look."

Juan paused outside a closed door on the other side of the passageway. "Hey, here's Cornero's office."

"Are you sure?"

Juan shot him an ironic look and gestured at the nameplate on the door.

ANTHONY CORNERO

> ~ *Bianca Finally Meets Miles Donahue*
> *in the Salle Blanche* ~

Bianca and her escort, Douglas Fairbanks, descended to the lower deck and followed their usher to the *Salle Blanche*. Ironic, since Blanche was her real name. They passed through the restaurant and down the long corridor to a large cabin at the end, where they met Charlie Chaplin in the passageway. He was friend and neighbor to both Doug and Bianca, though knowing his penchant for very young women, Bianca usually maintained a healthy distance between them. Since she was with Doug this evening and in the midst of a crowd, she let Charlie give her a kiss on the cheek. The two men hooked arms with her, and they entered the *Salle Blanche* as a unit. All eyes in the room turned toward them, three of the most famous people in the world.

The *Salle Blanche* was a long, luxurious hall that had been carved out of at least three regular-sized cabins. A bar that wound around two sides of the room was decorated with colorful mosaic tiles depicting a classical scene of Bacchus riding on a donkey, with a bunch of grapes in one hand and an overflowing wine chalice in the other. A glass door led to an outside terrace with two or three small tables, where tuxedoed men were just sitting down for intimate card games. Bianca hadn't seen an outside balcony from the ferry. This hall must be on the seaward side of the ship, she thought.

The *Salle Blanche* was well named, for aside from the artwork on the bar, the entire room was white—the walls, the tiled floor, the carved woodwork of the ceiling, the sparkling crystal and painted metalwork of the chandelier and the lamps. Even the leather on the chairs and the felt top of the large gaming table in the center of the room were white. As Charlie made his way over to take his seat at the table, Doug leaned over to whisper in Bianca's ear. "See the guy next to Chaplin in the double-breasted dinner jacket? That's Donahue."

Bianca examined her quarry. Donahue was a well put-together fellow, surprisingly young, she thought, to be a millionaire and the father of a grown woman.

"Evening, gents," Doug said, all affability. "I've agreed to introduce my friend Bianca to the joys of Texas Hold'em. She would like to observe the action for a hand or two, if you gentlemen don't object."

Bianca could tell by the smitten looks around the table that no one was going to object. Doug proceeded with the introductions. Eight people had settled in around the table, some of whom were familiar to her—producer Walter Wanger, screenwriter Ben Glazer, Harry Chandler, publisher of the *Los Angeles Times*, Chaplin—and some who were not, a retailer whose last name was Mann, a Long Beach councilman whose name she didn't get, a guy named Beale whose line of work she didn't get, Doug, and Miles Donahue the oilman. When his turn came, Donahue took her hand and she looked him in the eye, sizing him up.

A white-jacketed waiter came in to take their drink orders as the men seated themselves around the table and cut the cards to see who would deal first. Bianca took a seat behind Doug, next to the wall, and watched the interplay with interest. Cards were considered the work of the devil back in her little eastern Oklahoma hometown, so she hadn't been exposed to the art until she came to California and could hardly call herself an expert. It didn't take long to see who was rash and who was cautious, who knew what he was doing and who did not. Who was a gracious winner or a sore loser. Donahue turned out to be the latter. This struck Bianca as odd, since he won more than he lost, and even when he did lose, he could well afford it.

There was a lot of good-natured banter around the table, which Donahue cheerfully joined whenever he won a hand.

After one particularly lucrative win, Mr. Beale teased Donahue about the fairness of the house winning all his money. Donahue took the jibe with forced good humor. "Believe me, Beale, I have nothing to do with the running of this tub."

The opening was too fortuitous to pass up. "Are you part-owner of the *Monaco*, Mr. Donahue?"

He turned in his chair to look at her. "I am, Miss LaBelle,

though I am not involved in any way with the day-to-day workings of the casino. I am the most silent of silent partners."

"From the looks of things," Chaplin said, "your investment is going to pay off in spades."

"Let's hope so. In the meantime, what say you gentlemen let me try to win some of my money back? Deal, Mr. Chaplin."

Bianca wanted to ask Donahue if he was aware that Valentino had also been an investor, but the moment passed. The game resumed, and after an hour, the waiter reappeared to refill drinks between hands, and the players decided to take a short break. Since business could not be ignored for long, Wanger the producer cornered Doug to discuss a project, and Glazer, the screenwriter, made a beeline for Bianca to pitch a script before she could make her way around the table to Donahue.

"Yes, yes," she said, struggling to be gracious. "I'll look at it. Send it to my agent." Glazer may have wanted to say something else, but Bianca didn't give him a chance. She slipped out of his grip and sidled up to Donahue, who had lit a cigar and was puffing contentedly, still at the table, counting his chips.

"Mr. Donahue," she said. "Are you by any chance related to a young lady named Jenny Donahue?"

He winced as though she had slapped him. "How do you know Jenny? Do you know where she is?"

Bianca put on a surprised expression. "I don't know her. I was at the United Artists lot last week for a meeting with George Fitzmaurice. I mentioned to him that I'm looking for a private secretary, and he told me that I'd be well advised to offer the job to his former assistant Jenny Donahue. He told me that she was the best assistant he had ever had but had recently resigned from the studio, and he didn't know her forwarding address. I thought maybe if you knew her you could put me in touch with her."

Donahue stood up. He looked stricken. "Jenny's my daughter. We had a falling-out and now she refuses to talk to me. Or see me. So, no, I don't know where she is. If you find her, tell her to get in touch with her old man."

"Oh, I'm so sorry to bring up such a painful subject. You can be sure that if I ever do meet her, I will let her know I spoke to you. I had heard of Jenny before, you know. My late friend Rudy Valentino knew her and spoke well of her."

Donahue stiffened, and the fire that flared in his eyes caused Bianca to step back. She had suspected she might be poking the bear. She had been counting on the company to see that she didn't get eaten.

"Don't mention that damned wop's name to me," he said between clinched teeth.

Bianca put on her coolest face. "I beg your pardon?"

Donahue took himself in hand and drew in a breath. "Forgive my language, Miss LaBelle. Now, if you'll excuse me, there is something I need to do before the next hand." He stalked out of the cabin. Doug came up behind her and grasped her arm.

"What was that all about?"

"I don't know, but I intend to find out. He certainly didn't make any bones about hating Rudy."

"You'd better let me talk to him, my girl. He's more likely to spill his guts to another guy than he is to a girl he doesn't know."

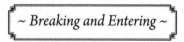

~ Breaking and Entering ~

As Oliver and Juan eyed the nameplate on Cornero's office door, a man in a white waiter's jacket clattered down the steps (ladder) at the end of the passageway. Oliver began belting out "Sweet Adeline," and Juan joined in as they staggered down the passageway with their arms over each other's shoulders, away from Cornero's office and toward the stairs. (Oliver could not make himself think of them as a "ladder.") The waiter shot them a disdainful glance as he passed but otherwise didn't ask them what the hell they were doing there. Oliver was right. This sort of thing happened all the time. The staff knew that the high rollers were to be indulged, even when they were boors and idiots. They carried on until the waiter disappeared into the kitchen, then returned to Cornero's office door and tried the handle. Locked. Oliver bent over to examine the locking mechanism in the lever that served as a doorknob.

"I'd force it for you, but bulkhead doors weigh a ton." Juan kept his voice low.

Oliver shook his head. Brute strength would certainly be ineffective against the steel door. He pulled a set of lock picks out of his pocket and knelt down. "Give me the high sign if you see anybody coming."

Juan leaned against the bulkhead with his arms crossed and tried to look nonchalant. Oliver had the door open in two seconds flat. Juan was impressed. "Hey, you're pretty good at that. Do a lot of breaking and entering, do you?"

"Lockpicking is the first thing they teach you at private eye school." Oliver slipped into the dark office, gesturing for Juan to follow. What little light there was in the cabin came from two portholes looking out over a black expanse of sea and a slightly less black, star-spangled sky. Oliver could make out a large square shape in the middle of the floor. He assumed it was a desk. He fumbled his way across the cabin and felt around over the desktop until he hit upon a lamp and switched it on. The door had a tight seal that would keep both water and light from leaking out into the corridor, and Oliver didn't care if a passing ship or a whale caught sight of them through the portholes. Cornero's office was utilitarian, containing nothing more than the oak desk, two plain wooden chairs, and a row of wooden filing cabinets beside the door. Oliver sat down and eyed the desktop. A blotter, a pen holder, a picture of a woman and a young boy. "Family man," Oliver muttered.

"What are we looking for?" Juan said.

Oliver placed both hands on top of the desk. "We don't have

time to do a thorough look, so I'm just going to get the lay of the land right now. If I see anything promising, I'll figure out a way to come back when nobody is around and have a leisurely gander. You go back out in the hall…"

"Corridor."

"…corridor and keep an eye out. I'll just take a minute to go through this desk and see what's what."

Juan did as he was told, and for a few minutes, the only sound in the cabin came from rustling paper and squeaking drawers as Oliver searched.

He found three long black ledgers in one of the side drawers and pulled them out for a quick examination. One was a manifest and payroll entries written in a neat, spidery hand. The second was a checkbook. The third, a fatter ledger, had several sections: inventory, accounts receivable, accounts payable, debit, and credit. Oliver flipped through quickly, wishing for all the world he had a miniature camera, or that he had the balls to just steal the thing. Since he had neither, he would report to Dix what he had seen tonight and let her decide what his next move would be. He expected she would be most interested in the ledgers. After all, it was a second set of books which had brought down her lieutenant, Mr. Ruhl. Careful bookkeeping was as important to criminals as it was to honest businessmen, but it was often a lot more dangerous if the wrong person got hold of the books.

He skimmed through the entries. The nightly take for the casino was eye-popping. So were the nightly expenditures. The heading on the very last page of the ledger was "Shareholders." The entries were listed in a typical double-entry fashion, debit on one side and credit on the other. Only three names were listed: Miles Donahue had supplied twenty thousand dollars; Jack Dragna had invested three times on three different dates to the tune of ten thousand a pop; Rudolph Valentino had contributed to Cornero's floating casino in five installments of different amounts ranging from five thousand to twenty-five thousand—much more than

Bianca had told Oliver about. None of the investors had realized any return, not yet. This was not surprising for such a new business. But the interesting thing about the debit column beside Valentino's name was that someone had penciled in "cancelled."

Either Cornero had already paid Valentino back in full, or now that he was dead, Cornero no longer worried about paying him back at all.

> ~ *Bianca works her Magic on*
> *Tony the Hat* ~

Bianca watched Doug chase after Donahue, who was heading down the corridor toward the restaurant. She intended to allow Doug a few minutes alone with Donahue before she interrupted. It was probably true that Donahue would speak more freely to another man, but Bianca considered this her murder investigation, and she was not going to let anyone usurp her role as chief interrogator. She watched as Doug caught up to Donahue at the entrance to the restaurant, but before she could follow, she was waylaid by Glazer again. His persistence was business as usual for Hollywood, and in other circumstances Bianca wouldn't have minded his flattering attention. She was on the verge of extricating herself from Glazer's company by means of some wildly inappropriate language when she was saved.

Tony Cornero himself was walking through the deck, greeting the gamblers and playing the gracious host. A tall, silent, bald bodyguard followed along in Cornero's wake. Tony locked eyes with Bianca, recognized her at once, and interrupted Glazer's monologue. "Good evening. I hope you are enjoying the house's hospitality, Miss LaBelle, Mr. Glazer."

Bianca thanked her lucky stars for the intrusion and slipped her arm through the crook of Cornero's elbow. "This is an amazing vessel you have here, Mr. Cornero. I would love a tour of the ship, if you have the time."

Bianca's sparkling green eyes, winsome smile, and gorgeous gams convinced Cornero that he had all the time in the world. "I would love to give you a tour, Miss LaBelle." They left Glazer standing in the corridor, fuming.

Bianca had recognized the notorious Tony Cornero from his pictures in the paper, and there had been plenty of them. The bootlegger was a young man, not yet thirty. He was attractive as well. He was of average height with thick black hair and an impish look in his black eyes. Cornero had been smuggling Canadian whiskey into Southern California with his fleet of freighters for only three years, but he was already spectacularly successful at it. He was the major supplier for clubs, restaurants, and moguls all up and down the coast, becoming a millionaire by the time he was twenty-five years old. Cornero's criminal enterprise was also a cozy family business. Tony's brother, Frank, and both his sisters were managing partners. The law had been after the Corneros since the first day they landed a shipment of whiskey on the beach, but thus far Tony had had smarter lawyers and faster speedboats. He had more trouble dealing with other gangsters than with the feds.

Tony showed off the beautiful movie star on his arm to the high rollers while he proudly showed off the beautifully decorated high roller cabins to her. He was a charming man, clever and full of jokes, and Bianca had to steel herself to keep from liking him.

"How come you decided to branch out into gambling ships, Mr. Cornero?" she asked. "Your importing business is doing so well."

He smiled at her choice of words. "Importing" sounded so much better than "smuggling."

"Please, call me Tony. You have to keep moving forward when you're in business, or you'll end up moving backwards. Prohibition has been great, but it won't last forever. Them knuckleheads in Congress will repeal it eventually, and when they do, I plan on already having another ace in the hole. The *Monaco* is my test case, Miss LaBelle. Running a floating casino for fat cats is all very well and good, but what I'd really like is to have an armada of gambling ships for regular Joes. You know, accountants and shop clerks and insurance salesmen. Honest games, no cheatin' anybody, just a good night out with your pals or with the wife. A game of cards, a good steak, dancing. Maybe even a show."

They passed through the restaurant, and Tony interrupted his narrative to show off the decor and comment on the French-inspired menu. Bianca did her best to appear fascinated and ignore Doug Fairbanks and Miles Donahue sitting with their heads together at a table in the corner.

After Tony had properly impressed her with the food offerings, he returned to the topic of his future plans as they walked toward the stairwell and down to the lower deck. "Just picture it, Miss LaBelle. A ship twice as big as this tub. One whole deck is a ballroom with a live band and a singer. Two shows a night. I'm thinking of hiring a comic—I know a guy who will make your sides split. None of them smutty jokes, either. Clean stuff a guy won't be embarrassed for his wife to hear." They stepped out of the stairwell onto the lower deck. "Now, this deck is closed to the public. It's mostly offices and crew cabins. Almost two hundred people work on the *Monaco,* fifty of them full time. Can you imagine? I had to have help to fill all the positions…" He gave her a sly wink. "…with honest workers, that is. Now, what I want to show you down here is the kitchen. Absolutely state of the art. It's located below the dining room, and we got dumbwaiters and an elevator right in the kitchen so that the servers don't have to climb up and down the stairs or even go out into the passageway."

He was waving his free arm about, pointing out this and that, but Bianca wasn't listening. She was distracted by the two men in tuxedos walking away from them, toward the stairs at the opposite end of the corridor.

Tony didn't seem to notice them, but the bodyguard (whose presence Bianca had forgotten) slipped around from behind his boss and followed the duo. By the time all three men had disappeared up the stairs, Tony was telling her more about his plans for the future. "I got a magician lined up too. He calls himself Fabulous Franz from Bavaria. What an act, him and his skinny little assistant, Gretel! You got to see this guy. I didn't want him to get away, get another gig before I got the new gambling ship outfitted, so I've got him working upstairs as a croupier. His hands move so fast that all you can see is a blur."

Something tickled in Bianca's brain. "A magician? You have a magician working for you?"

"I do. I'll tell you what, as soon as I show you this swanky kitchen, I'll take you up top and have him do a trick for you."

> ~ *Douglas Fairbanks had never seen*
> *the Ugly Side of Donahue before.*
> *He Did Not Enjoy the Sight.* ~

"She was my only daughter, the light of my life. She met 'Vasilino'—that's what I call him, the little greaser—at one of my fundraisers." Miles Donahue paused and fingered his glass thoughtfully. "But Jenny will be back. It's just a matter of time, now that the spaghetti-gargler is gone for good. I'm her father and she's my girl. She can't stay away from me forever."

Douglas Fairbanks leaned back in his chair, away from the miasma of misery that surrounded Miles Donahue. Fairbanks had worked with Donahue on charity projects and had played poker with him many times, as had Valentino. In fact, he would have sworn Valentino and Donahue had been friends, or at least friendly. After Donahue had stormed out of the *Salle Blanche*, Fairbanks had caught up with him quickly and suggested they join one another in the dining room for a drink and a chat. He had thought he'd have to persuade Donahue to tell him what had happened between himself and his daughter. He didn't have to persuade very hard. Donahue must have been about to burst with the need to talk, and who better to spill your guts to than Robin Hood himself?

"I saw them talking to one another at the gala and didn't think anything of it," Donahue said, "but then they left together. She said they only went for coffee, but he took her to luncheon the next day. I warned her about him, told I knew for a fact that he was a syphilitic, womanizing, half queer, Italian Bolshie who'd ruin her reputation and break her heart, but she wouldn't listen. I forbade her from seeing him. She defied me. I know because I put a tail on her. I locked her in her room, but one of the maids let her out. When Vasilino got involved with that Polish actress, things cooled off, and I figured that would be the end of it, but by that time Jenny was in such a lather she wouldn't speak to me. She said I ruined her life. I cut off her funds, but she got the job as Fitzmaurice's assistant. I knew they met up again while he was shooting that sheik movie. I tried to get Fitzmaurice to fire her, but he wouldn't do it. She told her mother that she loved him, Vasilino, that orchid. I couldn't stand the idea of him touching her. Putting his dirty hands on her."

His gaze wandered off and a feral look came over his face. "Then he died. Good riddance to bad rubbish. Jenny took it bad. She quit Fitzmaurice and told her mother that she was going to leave California, get a job back east where she could make a lot of dough fast and leave the country. I've got a bunch of guys trying to find her. I don't know where she is. She may have told her mother where she was going, I don't know. Angie isn't talking to me, either. She says I drove Jenny away."

For a long moment, Fairbanks said nothing. Such vulnerability from another man made him uncomfortable. To tell the truth, deep feelings of any sort made him uncomfortable. "I'm sorry, Donahue," he said. He had agreed to help Bianca try to locate the elusive Jenny by introducing her to Donahue, but this had turned out to be a dead end. Donahue didn't know where she was, either, and bringing up the subject had only managed to upset him. Fairbanks signaled the waiter. "Bring us a couple of whiskeys. And leave the bottle."

> ~ *Sleight of Hand, Illusions,*
> *Yet Has All Been Revealed?* ~

Cornero escorted Bianca to the main casino on the top deck, pausing at one gaming table after another to introduce her to anyone who was anyone. Bianca was growing annoyed at being shown off like a prize racehorse, but she bit her tongue, determined to endure at least long enough to get a gander at Cornero's magician-cum-croupier. Bianca tried to pretend she hadn't seen Jim Quirk wave at her when they passed him at the baccarat table. She didn't need a reporter sniffing around her tonight.

She scanned the room, looking for Oliver. She had recognized him as one of the men heading for the stairwell below decks. She didn't know the other man he had been with, the one posing as his valet, but she guessed Oliver had recruited him to help the investigation. Had they been snooping through the ship's offices? She had been a little worried when Cornero's man followed the two as they left the lower deck, but when she caught sight of Oliver sans his companion, standing at the roulette table and chatting with Jack Dragna, she relaxed. It was Oliver's task to investigate the gangsters, and she trusted him to know what he was doing.

"Miss LaBelle," Cornero said, "I'd like you to meet Fabulous Franz."

Bianca wrenched herself out of her reverie and extended a hand to the thin, dark-haired man dealing cards at the blackjack table. The dealer grasped it and nodded a greeting. "Excellent to meet you." He spoke with a heavy German accent.

"Franz, show the lady what you can do with a deck of cards," Cornero commanded.

What Franz could do was mind-boggling. Cards appeared

and disappeared before the astounded onlookers' very eyes as he shuffled faster than they could follow. He dealt four aces off the top, then four queens off the bottom. He called for a volunteer to name four random cards and produced those very cards from the deck in the order called. To begin with, Franz's only audience was Bianca and the gamblers already seated at the blackjack table, but as his tricks grew more and more fantastic, Franz drew a crowd.

Bianca paid little attention to Fabulous Franz's amazing feats of legerdemain. She was scrutinizing his eyes. One was brown. The other was gold.

She extricated herself from Cornero the moment the demonstration was over, making the excuse that she had to get back to her escort in the *Salle Blanche* before the next hand began. Cornero looked as though he would object, but he was interrupted by his bald bodyguard, who appeared out of the crowd and leaned in to whisper something in his ear.

While Cornero was distracted, Bianca sped toward the stairwell. She didn't dare speak to Oliver at the roulette table, not here among all these witnesses. The best she could do right now was find Doug as fast as possible and tell him what she had seen.

> ~ All things come to he who waits,
> Even a Punch in the Mouth. ~

Oliver and Juan had made their way back up top to the casino to wait for Oliver's seat at the table in the *Salle Blanche* to open up. They had managed their stealth surveillance mission without getting caught, but Oliver hadn't wanted to press his luck and spend too much time in Cornero's office. The lower deck was usually quiet on high rollers' night, but they could still be seen by someone with a lot of nasty questions about their presence.

Juan took up a position beside a potted palm and did his usual fading-into-the-background act, while Oliver wandered around the casino for a few minutes, checking out the action and trying to decide the best use of his time. His mind was made up for him when he saw Jack Dragna, Black Hand blackmailer, member in good standing of the Los Angeles mob, and the third investor in the *Monaco,* at the roulette table. He elbowed aside a woman in a blue sheath to stand beside the gangster.

Oliver put a hundred-dollar chip on black twenty-nine. He had no emotional investment in black twenty-nine, but it was next to red thirty, where Dragna had placed his chips. He lost on the first spin, as did Dragna, which gave him an excuse to commiserate. He lost another couple of Cs before gaining them back by betting on red even. Dragna won big on the third spin by sticking with his red thirty. After their shared good fortune, Oliver figured he had built up enough proximal camaraderie to offer to buy Dragna a drink.

Before he had a chance to issue the invitation, he felt a tap on his shoulder and turned to find himself face-to-face with Tony Cornero.

Cornero was sporting his most hospitable smile. "Mr. Nash, would you please come out on the promenade with me? There's something I'd like to discuss with you."

Jack Dragna raised an eyebrow. "What's up, Tony?"

"Just business, Jack." Cornero didn't take his eyes off of Oliver.

If he had had the chance, Oliver would have asked what subject Cornero could possibly want to discuss with a lumberman from Washington state, but the bald man's expression, not to mention the vise-like grip on his arm, stifled his inquiry. He cast a desperate glance toward the potted palm, but Juan was nowhere to be seen.

———

Bianca was halfway across the casino when she saw Cornero and his thug pull Oliver away from the roulette table and head outside. She paused mid-step, suddenly unsure of what to do. She was desperate to tell Doug about the magician whose eyes did not match. She did not want anyone to know of her association with Oliver, but she especially did not want K. D. Dix to know, and there were a number of people on this boat who'd be only too happy to spill the beans.

Whatever Cornero had wanted with Oliver, it didn't look good.

She could at least try and find out if her inside man was in trouble. If he needed help, she had the option to call on Douglas Fairbanks to stage a rescue, after all.

———

Once the bodyguard had propelled Oliver outside onto the promenade deck, Cornero turned to face him. The friendly expression he had put on in the casino had disappeared. "Who are you?"

"Oliver Nash from…"

"Don't give me that bullshit. My head of security here saw you come out of my office with your sidekick, who he recognized, by the way. Your gorilla is K. D. Dix's hatchet man. You work for Dix."

Oliver could feel the sweat pop out on his forehead. He figured his best bet was to make out like this was all a case of mistaken identity. "What the hell? What kind of joint is this? I come all the way down from Seattle and think I'm going to have a little fun and drop some dough on a night out and you sic Baldy on me? What do you want from me?"

"Don't make a fuss, Mr. Nash, or whoever you are. I'd hate for my associate to have to toss you overboard."

Oliver's options flashed through his mind. Most of them had the potential to end very badly. Swimming to shore three miles in what direction he didn't know, through shark-infested waters in pitch darkness, did not appeal.

Where the hell was Juan?

Baldy patted Oliver down, took his wallet out of his jacket and handed it to Cornero, who looked it over. "Well, well. A gumshoe. I'd heard that Dix had hired an op to find out what happened to her boob of a son. Looks like she decided to send you on a spying expedition. So, what does she want from me?"

"I don't know who you're talking about. I'm just here for..."

Cornero cut him off. "Spare me the lies. I ain't got all night." He turned to Baldy. "Take this *imbroglione* to the boiler room."

Oliver considered trying to fight his way out, but even if he managed to get away from Cornero, where would he go? He was on a ship. No matter where he hid, they'd find him eventually. His options narrowed to one when Baldy pulled out a .38 and pointed it at Oliver's belly.

Oliver threw up his hands. "All right, all right. Tell your torpedo to back off. We don't have to make a big deal out of this. We don't have to go anywhere, either. I'll tell you whatever you want to know."

"Don't worry, Mr. Nash, I ain't going to kill you. My associate here is just going to put you on ice for the rest of the evening and you and me are going to have a little talk. You'll still be in one piece when you leave for shore on the last ferry at dawn."

Baldy took the initiative and punched Oliver in the stomach. He doubled over, every molecule of air knocked out of his body, and struggled to draw breath before Baldy walloped him in the back of the head with the gun butt and knocked him senseless.

~ Bianca Calls out the Cavalry ~

It is hard to make a stealthy escape from a crowded room when you're famous. Bianca was accosted in a dozen ways as she hurried through the casino on her way to find Fairbanks. Several people called her name, and a few asked for autographs. People in the business wanted to talk to her. Twice she felt a hand pat her on the behind and someone tugged at her skirt as she passed a table. She ignored them all.

She gathered up her long skirt in one hand and skipped down the stairs, bursting onto the lower deck with such an agitated look on her face that when Fairbanks caught sight of her, he stood up from the table where he sat with Donahue, concerned. "What's wrong, Missy?"

The two men had made short work of the bottle of Canadian whiskey the waiter had brought them, and Bianca noticed that Fairbanks was a little tipsy. Still, he was in better shape than Donahue, who was passed out cold with his head on the table.

"Doug, it was Cornero! Cornero had Rudy killed." She gripped Fairbanks's arm, excited.

"What are you talking about?"

She leaned in to stage-whisper in his ear. "Remember how I told you that both Barclay Warburton and Jean Acker said that the imposter magician who poisoned Rudy had two different-colored eyes? Well, I just saw him. He works for Cornero! He's upstairs in the casino right now. Come on, come on!"

"Wait a minute, little lady. What do you think we are going to do about it right now, right here on Cornero's ship? We need to get out of here. There should be a water taxi leaving for shore in a few minutes. We have to go to the police or the feds."

Bianca was practically jumping up and down with impatience. "No, no, I know that. But first we have to help Oliver. Cornero and his hatchet man cornered him in the casino. I was able to follow them out onto the deck. It's dark and they didn't see me, so I hid beside a lifeboat and overheard them questioning him. Cornero knows that Oliver works for Dix. They smacked him in the head and dragged him off to the boiler room. Come on, Doug, I talked him into working for me on the sly. I can't let Cornero hurt him!"

Fairbanks covered his eyes with one hand. This is what happens when people mix you up with the parts you play, he thought. He dropped his hand and emitted a sigh. "Aw, shit. Well, come on then, let's try to rescue your boy."

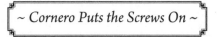

~ Cornero Puts the Screws On ~

It was impossible to know how much time had passed before Oliver began to swim back to consciousness, if one could call the images that drifted in and out of his awareness "consciousness." A sensation of movement, a rough surface under him. Was he being dragged across a floor? Wait, he had been on a boat. The deck? Then there was nothing but darkness for who knew how long, which finally gave way to the smell of something nauseating, like dead fish or rotting seaweed. Someone was saying something. In English, he thought, but his brain couldn't yet decipher what the words meant. A burst of pain in his head caused a lightning show of bright colors before his eyes as he was jerked up into a sitting position, and then more darkness.

With a mighty act of will, he tried to gain control of his muscles, but it was no use. His hands were immobilized behind his back. He was leaning against a narrow, metal object. He gulped in a lungful of fetid air, and his vision cleared enough for him to see that he was in a large, dark space. It was hot. It was noisy, a continual pulsing beat. It was damp. He was sitting in something wet, and he felt an instant of alarm before he realized that it was water and not his own blood. As his eyes accustomed themselves to the darkness, shapes began to appear. A maze of pipes. A metal gangplank overhead and metal stairs. Motors, pumps. He was somewhere deep in the bowels of the ship, sitting on a narrow walkway above two huge machines. Turbines? Generators? Oliver didn't know anything about ships. He couldn't guess how long he had been down here. His head was pounding, and his mouth felt like cotton. He tested his bonds and was dismayed to realize that he was tied to a pole of some sort.

This was a predicament.

His vision began to clear enough for him to make out two figures standing over him. One of them bent down to look him in the face. "Welcome back, Mr. Nash."

Cornero.

Oliver tried to speak, but he had no air. He gulped another breath and croaked, "You said you weren't going to hurt me."

"I said I wasn't going to kill you. You should pay better attention. Now, tell me what Dix is after and then you can lie here and rest in comfort for the rest of the night."

"All right, all right. She wants to know who rubbed out Valentino."

"Rubbed him out? I thought he died of a perforated ulcer."

"She seems to think different."

"Wait a minute. Are you saying Dix thinks I croaked Valentino? Why would I knock him off? He put up part of the money for this casino. In fact, he put up a wad to help me outfit this ship. He ain't going to help me anymore, is he?"

"You're not going to have to pay him back now, are you?" He could tell by Cornero's expression that this fact had already occurred to him. Oliver continued. "Besides, you have other backers, haven't you? Jack Dragna? Maybe Miles Donahue? I saw all three of you at Valentino's funeral."

"That don't mean I bumped off Rudy. I liked the little *paisan*. Besides, what does Dix care?"

"Who else knew that Valentino was one of your backers? Did somebody approach you with an offer once Valentino died?"

"Is that what this is all about? Dix wants to find out who I'm in business with? Why don't she just ask me?"

"Look, Tony, Dix doesn't share her thoughts with me. If I had to guess, I'd say she's interested in coming in on the business with you."

"She never was interested in nosing in on my import business before."

"But now you're expanding into gambling, and that's right up her alley."

Cornero considered this for a moment. "Dix could buy her own fleet of ships and have floating casinos up and down the whole Pacific coast. She don't need mine."

"Why should she start from scratch when you've already built this nice little establishment for her to get started with?"

"I wouldn't take a thin dime from K. D. Dix. Once she gets her claws into you, she never lets go."

No kidding, Oliver thought. "I imagine she's planning a hostile take-over. Even if you turn her down, once she finds out who your partners are, all she has to do is buy them out. And if they don't want to sell, she knows lots of very persuasive ways to change their minds."

Cornero listened with growing agitation, his face growing red. He took a breath to stave off an angry explosion. "Thanks for the warning, pal. Now you can take a message to Dix from me." He made a few filthy suggestions, then added, "And the next time I see one of her toadies on my ship, I'll send him back to her in little pieces." He slapped Oliver across the face for good measure, then turned to Baldy. "Tie him up good. I don't want him wandering around the ship." He stalked away and disappeared up the stairwell.

~ The Cavalry is on the Way! ~

The stairs changed from marble to metal as Bianca and Fairbanks descended into the bowels of the ship. When they reached the bottom deck, they found themselves standing on a narrow central landing with two huge iron hatches, one on either side of them.

"Which way?" Bianca was distressed.

"Usually the hold is fore, and the engine room is aft," Fairbanks said. "Did you hear them say they were taking Oliver to the hold or to the engine room?"

"No, Cornero said 'take him to the boiler room.'"

"That's the engine room. All right then, that side is the hold..." he gestured to his left, "so this door on the right is the one we want." Fairbanks heaved open the hatch, and they stepped through onto a small steel mesh platform that served as a landing for an upper level walkway around the deck. A metal ladder led down to the lower gangways. The engine room was dark, hot, and smelled of sea water and diesel. Far below them, Bianca could just make out several huge machines. The deep thrumming noise of engines and hiss of boilers made it difficult to think, much less to hear what was happening on the gangway below. But she could see Oliver tied to the railing and the bald man standing over him with a gun.

Bianca elbowed Fairbanks in the ribs and pointed. Fairbanks put a finger to his lips, and they communicated a quick plan to one another in an ersatz sign language though they probably could have shouted and not been heard below. Fairbanks took a small folding utility knife out of his trouser pocket and handed it to Bianca before he started down the ladder, and she crept around the upper walkway toward the opposite end of the deck.

———

Baldy's gleeful expression gave Oliver a bad feeling. "You don't have to hang around," he said to his captor, "I'm not going anywhere."

Baldy agreed. "No, you're not." He drew his .38 from his shoulder holster.

Oliver swallowed. "What are you doing? You can't kill me. Cornero said he wanted me to send a message to Dix. "

"Screw Cornero." Baldy pressed the gun to Oliver's temple. "I don't work for Cornero."

Oliver couldn't help but lean away from the gun barrel. "Dragna..." he managed. "Black Hand."

Baldy laughed. "Dragna's a *putz*. No, I seen the goon you're with. I know he's Dix's man. I got a dozen guys looking for him, and when we find him, he can take your head back to Dix. That's a message she'll listen to."

"Wait! I got a right to know who is..."

Oliver was interrupted by clatter on the gangway and Baldy spun around to see a man tripping toward them unsteadily.

It was Douglas Fairbanks in the flesh, complete with trim mustache and gleaming smile, apparently dead drunk. "Pardon me, old man." He had to yell to be heard over the engine noise. "I must have taken a wrong turn. Where's the poop deck?"

Oliver couldn't decide whether to laugh or cry. Baldy's back was to him now, so he couldn't see the thug's face, but he could imagine his shocked expression. What now? Shoot a famous movie star?

Maybe. Baldy decided to brazen it out. "Well, look who we have here. Ain't this a treat! Are you lost, Mr. Fairbanks? If you are, you'd better go back up them stairs and get unlost real fast. This don't have nothing to do with you, so keep your mouth shut about what you saw."

Fairbanks stopped in the middle of the gangway and threw his hands up in a gesture of compliance. "Now, hang on, old fellow." He paused to peer at the pistol in Baldy's hand. "Wait a minute. What's going on here?"

Oliver was riveted by the scene. It took him a moment to realize that Bianca had dropped down beside him from the walkway above. She was in her stocking feet, and as she crouched down, the slit in her skirt parted, baring one leg all the way up to her garter, from the top of which glinted the handle of a small Browning pistol. She slipped Fairbanks's knife out of her décolletage and cut through the cord that bound Oliver's hands.

Oliver was in danger of his life, and all he could think about was that Bianca was armed to the teeth in the sexiest possible way.

Fairbanks took a step backward, away from Baldy. "Say, old fellow, what have I stumbled on here?"

Baldy made a decision. "You, Fairbanks, get over here. You can keep my pal company for a while until I parlay with the boss about what to do with you. Can't have you blabbing."

Fairbanks appeared to have trouble understanding the gravity of the situation. "Blab about what?"

Oliver gestured for Bianca to hide before Baldy turned and saw her. She ignored him and stood up. He tugged on her skirt, mouthed, *You're not helping.* She slapped his hand away. Oliver tried to stand as well but a shock of pain from his head wound knocked him on his ass.

Fairbanks yelled, trying to draw Baldy's attention, but it was too late. Baldy to spun back around and leveled his .38 at Bianca. With no time to think of an alternative, Fairbanks gritted his teeth and sent a roundhouse kick to Baldy's head and sent him reeling over the side of the walkway. Baldy snatched at the railing but couldn't hold on. He made no sound as he fell, bounced off a turbine, and with a dull metallic thud, hit the deck far below.

Fairbanks looked down on Baldy's still form with a mix of astonishment and delight. "Hot damn!"

> ~ *A Close Shave!*
> *But there's no time to Savor their Escape.*
> *Worse Danger is Yet to Come!* ~

Fairbanks looked like a ton of bricks had just fallen on him, as surprised at what he had done as Baldy had been.

"Doug!" Bianca cried out and pointed to the landing above.

Miles Donahue was standing at the rail, stone sober. The gun he was pointing at Fairbanks's back was no .38, but a Colt revolver the size of a small cannon.

Oliver got to his knees, which wasn't easy. He was dizzy and stiff, and entirely confused. Bianca moaned.

Fairbanks's eyes widened as he looked back over his shoulder. "You?"

Donahue laughed. "Actors! What a couple of maroons! How kind you were to listen to my tale of woe, Fairbanks. And then you, you little bitch, came flitting up and the two of you made your ridiculous rescue plan right over my head. I heard every word. You think Cornero killed Vasilino? Hah! Cornero couldn't kill anybody. He's a simpleton who doesn't know the first thing about running a business. Why, that idiot couldn't find his dick on a dark night. Who do you think is in charge of hiring all the personnel for this rust bucket? Me, that's who."

Bianca gasped. "You're the one who hired Fabulous Franz to poison Rudy?"

"Don't say that pansy boy's name! They all work for me, all of them, my army of enforcers, accountants, waiters, poisoners, assassins. They do whatever I tell them, including get rid of the trash."

"So you had him poisoned?" Fairbanks said. "What a way to kill a guy. Why not have one of your punks shoot him?"

Donahue shrugged. "I tried to pull off a couple of 'accidents' but that didn't work. I didn't want to make him a martyr in my daughter's eyes. Besides, I wanted him to suffer."

Oliver dragged himself to his feet and took a few steps forward, positioning himself between Donahue and Bianca. "How are you going to get out of this, Donahue? Kill two of the most famous people on earth?"

"Yes, well, it's a shame, isn't it? The ferry is going to sink and take LaBelle and Fairbanks and some nameless schmuck to the bottom of the bay. The sharks'll probably get to the bodies before the cops can dredge them up in time to count the bullet holes. Now that you've eliminated Foster, I'll have to get one of my other..."

~ A Shot Rings Out! ~

It took Oliver a fraction of a second to realize that he was still alive. There had been loud report, a cry, a metallic ping, and ricochet, a clatter as Donahue's .45 went over the side of the rail and hit the deck below.

Oliver turned toward the source of the shot, behind him, trying to process what he saw. Bianca was standing at the end of the gangway, pointing her Browning over Oliver's head at Donahue, who was gripping his wrist and spewing the most spectacular invective at her.

She had shot the Colt out of his hand. Until that moment, Oliver thought that was only possible in movies and Western novels.

"Bianca!" Oliver cried out her name without thinking. Fairbanks rushed toward them, crying, "Run!"

It was too late to run. Bianca fired at Donahue again, and missed.

Donahue disappeared through the hatch, blood dripping from the wounded right hand hanging useless at his side.

Oliver sat down heavily on the walkway, and Bianca knelt down beside him. "Are you all right?"

Am I? Oliver wondered, but he said, "What the hell just happened? Donahue had Valentino killed because of his daughter?"

Bianca's green eyes were wild, and her face was flushed from excitement, fear, and the steamy heat of the boilers. "I thought it was Cornero! But it didn't have anything to do with money or gambling debts or bootlegging or any of that. Donahue's daughter had the hots for Rudy, and the feeling may have been mutual. So Donahue had Rudy poisoned to keep him away from his daughter. The question is what are we going to do about it?"

Fairbanks had crouched beside Bianca and put a protective arm around her. "We're not going to do anything about it, Missy. We're going to find a way to get the hell off this ship as fast as we can. You heard what Donahue said. Everybody on the boat works for him."

~ A Perilous Getaway ~

Oliver allowed Bianca and Fairbanks to help him to his feet, and the three headed for the hatch. If Donahue managed to alert his goons and send them down the ladder after them before they reached an upper deck, they'd be trapped. But it was the only exit from the boiler room that they could see, so they had no choice.

Fairbanks led the way, with Bianca behind him and Oliver limping along behind. He almost ran into Bianca when she balked at the foot of the ladder. "My shoes…" she said. "I left them on the walkway."

Fairbanks bounded up the steps without a backward look. "You can afford to buy new ones, Missy. Let's go! *Ándale!* Chop chop!"

She grumbled but obeyed, and the sight of her supple feet and slender ankles on the stairs before him almost made Oliver forget his aching head. They had just reached the deck above when they heard the clatter of feet rushing down the stairwell. Fairbanks shoved Bianca through the hatch ahead of Oliver and himself, and the three pressed their backs to the bulkhead, holding their collective breath, until several muscle-bound shapes bounded past the opening, headed toward the boiler room. When the footfalls faded, the fugitives slipped back onto the stairwell and continued upward.

They made it to the promenade deck and around the port side, where the water taxi docked or cast off every half hour to ferry passengers to and from shore. They were lucky. A taxi was tied up at the floating dock, loading a few listless gamblers who were either ready for bed or too skint to play another hand. They made their way down the wooden stairs to the landing, where the pilot gave them all a dubious once-over as he handed Bianca onto the boat.

"How long before you leave?" she asked.

"Five minutes, Miss." The pilot recognized Fairbanks and LaBelle, but their bruised companion and the bedraggled state of their couture caused him to raise an eyebrow. He had been ferrying Hollywood-types long enough not to be surprised at anything, so no questions were forthcoming.

The three escapees went as far aft on the ferry as possible, behind the passenger cabin, and flopped down on a bench.

Wedged between the two men, Bianca blew out a relieved breath. Donahue's gangsters could still spot them before the ferry left, but it was unlikely that anyone would make a move against them with so many witnesses around.

"Look at my dress," Bianca groused. "I knew that stupid slit skirt was a bad idea. It's torn almost up to my hip. And look at this oil spot. And my stockings!" She pooched out her bottom lip. "I paid a fortune for those shoes."

Fairbanks thought her complaints were hilarious, but Oliver was not so sanguine. "What is it with you two and those ridiculous moves down in the boiler room? This isn't one of your adventure flicks, and Donahue's killers aren't paid to let you win. You could have got us all killed!"

Fairbanks grunted. "Oh, shut up, Oliver, you ingrate. Bianca saved your life. Believe me, I would have let them have you. Besides, what else should we have done? Stood there and let them shoot us?"

Bianca came to Oliver's defense. "He's still in shock, Doug. He doesn't mean anything." She seized Oliver's arm and gave it a shake. "How do you think we do all those stunts you see on the screen, Ted? Doug is a tremendous athlete. He has the best physical trainers in the world."

Fairbanks preened a bit at her praise. "You're no slouch in that department yourself, little Missy. And that shot! Where'd you learn to shoot like that? Back on the farm at your daddy's knee?"

"I didn't even know a shot like that was possible," Oliver agreed.

An ironic glint lit Bianca's eyes. "I'd love to tell you I'm just that good. I was aiming for his head."

Their luck held. The taxi cast off just as Cornero himself appeared at the railing. He yelled something, but they couldn't make it out over the noise of the boat's motors.

"Now what?" Bianca said to no one in particular. "My goodness, I can't believe how far Donahue was willing to go just to keep his daughter and Rudy apart. Is he going to make sure we all die mysterious deaths, like Rudy did?"

Fairbanks mopped his forehead with his handkerchief. "Not if we get to the cops first."

Oliver made a skeptical noise. The "richer of two evils" bought the most police cooperation these days. "We'd be better off to go to the feds. They'd like nothing more than a good excuse to conduct a raid on Cornero and arrest all his business partners. Or they could nail Donahue for kidnapping."

"What about the three-mile limit? I thought the *Monaco* is outside of federal jurisdiction."

"They could come up with something, Bianca, maybe resurrect some long-forgotten law about piracy on the high seas."

She thought about this. "I do know a U.S. Marshal," she mused aloud.

"You do?" Oliver said. She never failed to surprise him.

Fairbanks laughed. "She's a pip, ain't she?"

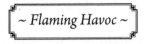

~ *Flaming Havoc* ~

When they reached shore and disembarked onto the floating dock, they stood in an uncertain little group as the rest of the ferry passengers made their way to their autos.

"Ted, I think you need a doctor," Bianca said. "Why don't you come home with me and I'll see you're taken care of?"

"I can't, Bianca. I don't know what happened to Juan—the guy that Dix sent out to keep an eye on me. He's bound to get back to shore eventually. He drove me out here in one of Dix's cars. I don't want him to see us together or know that we know one another."

"I can't just leave you here on the beach like this. Not after we went to such trouble to save you."

Oliver was touched by her concern, but he said, "Don't worry about me. I'll get home one way or another."

Raised voices and a flurry of activity on the ferry boat interrupted their conversation.

"What's going on?" Fairbanks said to a sailor who had jumped onto the dock to throw off the bowline.

The sailor didn't pause. "The *Monaco's* on fire!" he called as he rushed past them. "They're evacuating the passengers onto the lifeboats and we're going back to help."

The *Monaco* was three miles out to sea, but they could see an eerie glow on the horizon. Bianca raised her hands to her cheeks, horrified. "Oh, my God! All those people!"

"Is there anything we can do?" Fairbanks asked the sailor.

"Don't worry, sir." The sailor jumped back onto the water taxi as the motors revved. "The captain radioed that the evacuation is going well. We'll get everybody off." The boat pulled away into the night. The glow on the horizon expanded.

"What could have happened?" Bianca said. "Could a bullet have punctured a gas line?"

"We need to get you out of here, Missy, before Donahue lands." It took a few minutes for Fairbanks to convince Bianca to come with him, but Oliver would not be persuaded to leave, not just yet.

He waited on the beach all night as one after another, water taxis and lifeboats and civilian pleasure craft discharged their tuxedoed and gowned passengers, most of whom were well lubricated and behaving as though this were all a big adventure. He saw Cornero come in on the very last lifeboat, covered with soot, his hair singed, and clutching a large satchel as though it were a baby. Tonight's profits, Oliver thought. Oliver faded back into the crowd as Cornero disembarked and walked up and down the beach checking on the welfare of his crew and staff, for which Oliver gave him grudging credit.

Great, he thought. Now I've got Tony the Hat on my case. At least Cornero hadn't seen Bianca's part in all this. Oliver's biggest worry now was how to deal with Miles Donahue, infinitely rich, infinitely vindictive, and willing to kill to get his way. But Miles Donahue never landed, not with the rest of the rescued passengers, anyway.

Neither did Juan.

Oliver had no key for Dix's auto, so he left it in the parking area and hitched a ride into Long Beach, where he called a cab to take him home.

~ Aftermath ~

As soon as he was escorted into Dix's parlor the next morning, Oliver checked the corner, next to the lamp, but Juan was not there. A tall redhead with a snub nose stood in his place. Dix liked her bodyguards young and good looking.

Oliver had dragged into Santa Monica well after sunrise and had only taken time to change his clothes, wash his face, and put a bandage over the cut on his forehead before driving across Los Angeles to Pasadena to deliver his report to Dix. He was loopy from lack of sleep, but he had no intention of waiting for her to send someone after him. Best to get it over with.

He related the events of the previous night, editing out any reference to Bianca LaBelle or Douglas Fairbanks, and she had listened intently, only allowing herself a brief smile when he told her that he shot the gun out of Donahue's hand. He told her that after his escape, he had stood on the beach all night, watching the lifeboats land, but Donahue had not appeared.

She nodded. "But you saw Cornero?"

"Yes, I saw him. Dragna made it out, too. I heard on the radio this morning that Donahue is missing and presumed lost, but the rest of the passengers and crew made it out. The *Monaco* burned right down to the waterline. It's a total loss."

Dix did smile then, a broad, devilish grin. "I guess now that Donahue and Valentino are gone, Cornero will need a new business partner if he wants to outfit another gambling ship."

Oliver felt the blood drain out of his face and he swayed on the couch. He should have known. He should have figured it out. "That's why you sent Juan," he blurted. "Once I got the names of Cornero's investors, Juan's job was to eliminate them."

It took Dix a moment to figure out who he was talking about. "Oh, you mean Vlad. Vlad's job was to use his initiative. Apparently, he did."

"What about Jack Dragna?" he said.

She made a dismissive gesture. "Pfft. Jack and I understand one another. By the way, did you see what happened to Vlad?"

So his name was Vlad. "I don't know what happened to him. I never saw him again after Cornero nailed me. I figure that if he managed to get off the ship, he'd have made his way back to you. Donahue's punk told Cornero that he recognized Juan... Vlad... and knew he worked for you. Your boy probably has taken up residence at the bottom of the Pacific, along with Donahue."

Dix nodded, unaffected. Dead bodyguards were the price of doing business. "Too bad. He was good. Effective without any fuss."

Oliver sighed. "Did he have any family?"

"No. Just a cousin who works at the fishery over in Corona. Maybe he wants a job." She looked thoughtful. "You look done in, Ted." Dix was always so solicitous, so motherly toward him. "You had better go home and get into bed."

> ~ *Love is Dangerous,*
> *but Hatred is Exhausting* ~

Dix was overcome with momentary fatigue and poured herself a shot of whiskey. Her plan had worked out better than she expected. She had figured that it would take a while to eliminate Cornero's backers once she knew who they were. She hadn't planned on the *Monaco* burning. Now she would have start from scratch to outfit her own fleet of gambling ships. However, she didn't have to deal with Cornero if she didn't want to. She was sorry to lose Vlad, but Oliver had worked out all right. He was a competent investigator. She'd use him for side jobs again.

She didn't know why she felt low. That had been happening

more and more lately, tiredness that came upon her suddenly and for no particular reason. Well, maybe there was a reason. A few months earlier, when Oliver had discovered that her second-in-command, Mr. Ruhl, had been stealing from her for years, the betrayal had taken something out of her. Ruhl… If she had ever trusted anyone in her life, it was Ruhl. That's why she had to kill him. No matter what you feel for somebody, you mustn't ever let them get away with betraying you.

Funny. It didn't bother her nearly as much when Oliver turned up evidence that her own son had been involved in Ruhl's embezzlement scheme. Graham had always been a disappointment. Had she loved her boy? She didn't know. She tried. She wanted to love him. The truth was that five years earlier, after he disappeared without a word, Dix had been quietly relieved to be rid of his troublesome presence. At the time, she told herself that he had run afoul of somebody dangerous and gone on the lam, even though she suspected he had met a bad end. She had tried to find him but not very hard. When his skeleton had finally turned up on the beach a few months ago, she wasn't surprised.

But she'd never rest till she found his killer. Mercy could be the end of you in this dangerous way of life, especially if you were a woman.

She poured herself another shot and chugged it. Bracing. She was feeling much better. Fortunately, the weariness never lasted long.

Photoplay's beloved managing editor, James R. Quirk, passed away from pneumonia and heart disease on August 1. The following interview with Bianca LaBelle is the final article that Mr. Quirk wrote, a mere two weeks before his death:

I have followed Bianca LaBelle's career from the moment she burst upon the Hollywood scene in 1921 with her first Bianca Dangereuse film, *The Golden Goblet*, through her successful transition to the talkies, to her recent Academy Award nomination for *The Borgia Woman*. I met with Bianca early in July at her estate in Beverly

Hills to discuss her latest project, the formation of a new production company called Cherokee Pictures.

I spent two hours with Miss LaBelle, had a wonderful time, learned everything about her philosophy of moviemaking and her expanding media empire, and learned nothing at all about Miss LaBelle herself. Bianca LaBelle is smart, witty, and fun to be with. But Bianca LaBelle is a sphinx. She's a fine actress who never talks about her art. The expressive beauty of her eyes, soulful glance, her poise, all lend to her allure. Perhaps it is true that men are intrigued by a mysterious woman, and I believe that Bianca is mysterious because she knows all about herself and does not care to share any of it. She says nothing of her childhood other than it was a happy, healthy one, but there is a sadness about her that makes me wonder if she hit rock bottom before she came up again. The heights, now that she is among them, can't kid her. An intelligent person learns something from each mistake. The next time she knows what to avoid. I have known Bianca for years, but I have never met the real Bianca LaBelle.

———

Bianca sighed and closed the magazine. The rest of the article consisted of her talking about the pictures that she wanted to produce—artful, well-written pieces that would never be financed by the big studios—and Jimmy Quirk trying to wrangle personal information out of her, like he always did. She had become an expert in ways to dodge his questions.

Jimmy's unexpected death had been a shock. The official word was that he had died of bronchial pneumonia complicated by a weak heart, but she knew that his years of heavy drinking hadn't helped anything. In fact, he had had a bit of a buzz on when he came to Orange Garden to interview her for this very article. He was hardly drunk enough to notice, but tipsy enough to lower his inhibitions about broaching uncomfortable subjects.

They had been sitting in her living room, next to one another on her white couch. The interview was over. He had closed his steno pad and returned it to his briefcase. She had stood to show him to the door, when he said, "You know, August 23 marks the sixth anniversary of Rudy's death."

She sat back down, curious to know what was on his mind. "I'm well aware, Jimmy."

"Did you love him, Bianca?"

"I did, in my way. He was easy to love."

"I guess you've heard all the rumors that have popped up about his death in the last few years. About him being murdered and all."

"I'd have to be blind and deaf not to."

"Do you believe it?"

"What, that he was murdered? What if I did? What good would it do to dredge that all up now? How could anything be proven after all this time?"

Quirk leaned forward, a conspiratorial look on his face. "I know something about that, you know."

Bianca hadn't thought about the circumstances surrounding Rudy's death for years. She thought she was over the trauma of it all, but Quirk's statement caused her heart to skip. "What are you talking about?" How could Quirk know that Miles Donahue had had Rudy murdered? Quirk had been aboard the *Monaco* when Donahue died. When she had asked him to help her find Jenny, had she inadvertently put him on the murderer's trail? It's always a mistake to involve reporters in anything, she thought.

Quirk seemed to regret his comment at once. He leaned back

into the cushions and put a finger to his lips. "Never mind. I should have kept my head closed."

"Oh, come on, Jimmy. You can't say something like that and leave me hanging. What do you think you know about how Rudy died?"

"Nothing. Really. I just had a theory and nosed around a little. Maybe I'll tell you someday. Maybe not. I will say this, though. You ought to talk to George Ullman. If anybody knows what really happened to Rudy, it's him."

He refused to say any more. He left for New York shortly thereafter and she never saw him again. As for George Ullman, he was living on the East Coast with Beatrice. She had not spoken to him in ages.

A few weeks after Jimmy died, his wife, May Allison, who had given up acting and become a scriptwriter, moved back to California. In fact, Bianca and her little dog, Jack Dempsey, had paid a condolence call on May only the day before the *Photoplay* piece was published.

The women had spent a pleasant few hours telling each other amusing stories about Jimmy. He had been such a fixture in the entertainment industry, had known everybody, had an opinion about everything and wasn't shy about sharing it. Few of the current entertainment journalists, if you could call them "journalists," had nearly the class that Jimmy had.

When Bianca finally stood to leave, May handed her a sealed letter with her name on it. She recognized Jimmy's bold handwriting.

"What's this?"

"It's a letter for you from Jimmy. Something he wanted you to know. Don't open it now. Wait until you get home."

"For me? How odd. Do you know what's in it?"

"I don't," May said. "He gave me the envelope a few days before he died. But I swore upon the soul of my mother that I'd never, ever, open it. He also told me that I can't ever tell anyone that the letter even exists. And you must swear the same."

"Goodness, May…"

May held up a hand. "Never, never, ever."

Bianca had sworn, then tucked the letter into the big orange satchel she normally carried instead of a purse, where it had lain unread for several days.

———

Bianca put on her biggest, floppiest sun hat and her dark glasses, bundled Jack into her roadster, and drove to Casa del Mar near Santa Monica for a walk on the beach. The little pooch was ancient now, but even if he couldn't walk very far without a rest, he still loved to nose around in the sand. While the dog explored the detritus washed up by the surf, Bianca sat on a towel under a beach umbrella, watching a group of children playing on the beach.

There were four children in the group, ranging in age from around three to maybe ten years old. They resembled one another, dark-haired and long-limbed, very much like the woman keeping an eagle eye on them from her beach chair.

The children were building a sandcastle, and it seemed they were having a difference of opinion about its construction. One of the boys stood up and kicked a chunk out of a turret. Shrieks and yelling ensued, quickly nipped in the bud by a stern word from mother. Peace restored, the boy sat down and building resumed as though nothing had happened.

Bianca was overcome by a wave of nostalgia. Siblings. Sometimes she missed her own big, raucous family and her snug, loving place in it. Sometimes it was lonely not living amidst a tribe who would always take your side, whether you deserved it or not.

But everything had turned out all right. She was still young and beautiful, wealthy and famous, and had learned to use all those God-given advantages to get practically anything she wanted. She loved being in the movies, loved acting, loved pretending to be a queen, a businesswoman, a sorceress, a saint. Anyone other than herself. Everything had turned out all right, and it might not have.

In fact, it very nearly hadn't. She had run away from home when she was just a girl, given up everything she knew in her pursuit of fame and adventure. Then she had gotten pregnant at fifteen, abandoned by a faithless lover who sold her to a whorehouse in Arizona. But she had avoided that awful fate by engineering her own escape. She had had to give up her son, but he was being raised in a loving home by her sister in Oklahoma, and she was still able to be in his life. A dozen years earlier, her rash decision had changed everything. There was no going back now. She could never return to her former life, to who she was before. That way of life was closed to her forever. She had closed that door herself.

Still, she had reconciled with her family, apologized to her parents for causing them such distress by running away from home without a word, and they seemed to have forgiven her. They would never want for anything material again, not if she had anything to say about it. Yes, everything had turned out all right. That's what she told herself.

She still had her friends, though she had lost several over the past few years. Some had simply disappeared out of her life, like Pola Negri, and some had died, like Rudy, and now James Quirk. Jimmy had been such a presence in the entertainment industry that it was hard to accept that she would never see him again.

She heaved a sigh and rummaged through her satchel until she found the envelope that May had given her. Jimmy had written her name on the front of the envelope—*Bianca*—that was all. For a few moments, she simply held it in her hand, wondering if he had written farewell notes to several of his friends after he realized he was going to die, then given them to May to distribute.

She ran a finger under the flap and withdrew the letter. One typewritten page, single-spaced.

"Bianca,

"Back in 1926, after you and I met at the funeral home in

New York after Valentino died, my newsman's nose began to twitch. Early the next year, I began my own investigation into what happened to our mutual friend, and the plot that I uncovered is beyond belief. Yet I have kept my secret and told no one, not even May. I have not even mentioned it to George Ullman, who I am sure was the instigator of the scheme. I've violated every journalistic instinct I have to keep this secret, for this is information that would blow the lid off Hollywood and make me the most famous journalist in the United States and maybe the entire world. But I guess I have a soul, after all, because in the end, I decided that a man's life is worth more than headlines..."

———

Fee was deadheading the faded roses from the bushes in front of Orange Garden when Bianca's roadster came tearing up the drive and screeched to a halt at the front door, sending gravel flying. Bianca emerged from behind the wheel, white-faced and breathing heavily.

"What on earth has happened?" Fee demanded, alarmed.

Bianca handed over Jack Dempsey. "Fee, I just got the most unexpected news. I have to telephone George Ullman. Right now!"

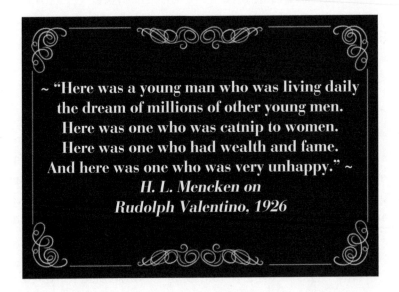

~ "Here was a young man who was living daily
the dream of millions of other young men.
Here was one who was catnip to women.
Here was one who had wealth and fame.
And here was one who was very unhappy." ~
H. L. Mencken on
Rudolph Valentino, 1926

When Bianca had boarded the airplane in Los Angeles, it was summer. When she stepped out onto the tarmac in Santiago, three days, four countries, two airlines, and one frighteningly bumpy ride in a bush airplane later, it was winter, chilly and wet, and she was stiff, tired, and rattled.

She had been to Santiago before, but not since the latest dictatorship had ended and the Chilean congress had taken power after a relatively peaceful coup. She remembered it as a beautiful, prosperous city, but the worldwide financial collapse two years earlier had wrecked Chile's economy as badly as it had that of the United States, so she was nervous about what she would find.

What passed for a terminal looked just the same as far she

could tell, plain and square but peaceful. As for Santiago, she'd have to reserve judgment, since the airstrip where she had landed was more than twenty miles outside the city.

She saw him standing on the tarmac with an umbrella in his hand. He looked older, more rugged than when she had last seen him healthy. He was well-dressed in a serge suit and a blue wool beret with a white silk scarf around his neck. The years had been good to him.

He came up to her as she stepped onto the runway and kissed her on the cheek. "Hello, *cara*. You are more beautiful than ever."

"Hello, Rudy. So are you."

"You must call me Raffaello now. Raffaello Guillermo."

She smiled. "Guillermo. Spanish for Williams."

"I had to choose a name I would remember," he said with a shrug.

After she had her passport stamped by an officious person in a blue uniform, Rudy walked her to his sturdy Daimler, parked in the dirt lot next to the terminal, and deposited her one valise in the trunk. He held the passenger door for her, then walked around to the driver's side and got in. They sat in silence for a long moment, taking in the sight of one another, before Bianca surprised herself by bursting into tears.

"How could you, Rudy?" she sobbed. "How could you do this to me, to all of us who love you?"

He could barely understand her through the tears. "Do not cry, my darling." He leaned across the seat and put his arms around her. "I had to give up everything and everyone, all my friends, even my brother and sister, all but my Jenny. Surely you can see why. Only George knows, and Beatrice, and the wonderful Dr. Meeker, who has now died. Even Mr. Campbell, the mortician, was told that my body was cremated at the hospital and a wax reproduction of my body was to be displayed to my grieving public. George told me that Campbell was only too happy to do it for the publicity. I was frightened when I received your wire and learned that Jimmy had discovered my secret and nosed out my hiding place, but he was a true friend and carried the secret to his grave. Now you are the only other person on earth who knows that Valentino lives."

Bianca's tears had abated. She extricated herself from Rudy's grasp, mopped her face and wiped her runny nose with a lacy handkerchief. "Oh, I know, Rudy. I do understand. And I am your true friend as well and will never tell. Fee thought I had lost my mind when I suddenly insisted on leaving town in the middle of a contract negotiation for a vacation in Chile."

"How is Fee?"

"Doing wonderfully. In love, I think! But now you must tell me about your new life. You finally own a farm?"

He started the auto and pulled out onto the road. "I do. All of my dreams have been fulfilled. My Jenny and I—oh, I cannot wait for you to know her. You will love one another. My Jenny and I rent a bungalow in Santiago, but we have a wonderful farm south of Mendoza, three days' drive from here, across the border in Argentina. You must see it while you are here. I grow grapes, *cara*, and Merino sheep. Both my wool and my wines are of the best quality. Also, we have two boys now. Gianni is five and Antonio is two. Many Italians live in the region, so I feel at home. As for Jenny…" he chuckled, "for her, it has been a challenge, but she tells me she would not change our life for anything in the world."

"But you were so ill! The last time I saw you in the hospital, you were unconscious and raving."

"I was ill. But when the good doctor told me I would live, I decided I could no longer go on being the great screen lover. I had George contact Jenny on the West Coast, and she came to be with me in New York. The good doctor gave me drugs and I went to sleep. Jenny nursed me for a long time in Brooklyn, in a house the Ullmans rented for us. When I recovered, George helped me do what I had to do to become Raffaello, and we came here."

"Do you keep up with your family? You know that Alberto and Maria are suing George for mismanaging your estate? They told the probate court that eighty thousand dollars' worth of your property and goods have gone missing, so the judge removed George as executor and appointed someone else."

"Yes, George keeps me informed. Poor George," Rudy said with a laugh. "He sent that money to me, you know. That is enough to last for the rest of my life—this life, my real life. Well, George is glad to be rid of the responsibility, I am sure. Do not worry about him. He was well compensated for helping us to escape."

"I assume Jenny knows that her father's body was found in the wreckage of the *Monaco* a few days after it went down. The coroner found no water in his lungs, so they think he died before the ship sank."

"Yes. She was heartbroken, you can imagine. Even after we knew it was he who tried to kill me. Especially after that. He was her father, after all."

"The irony is that Donahue died believing that he had finally gotten rid of Rudolph Valentino. But you did that yourself." Bianca removed her cheerful, rust-colored slouch hat and settled back for the long road trip into Santiago. "Well, I have to hand it to you. You pulled it off. And now that Rudolph Valentino is dead and Raffaello Guillermo has taken his place, tell me the truth. Was it worth it? Are you happy?"

The gleaming smile that Bianca remembered so well lit up his face. "*Cara*, I am so happy you cannot know. I have my farm, my Jenny, my children, that is all I need. And what of you, my darling? I read of your fame, your adventures, even here at the end of the earth. But still you keep your life a mystery. Tell me, what happened to your detective friend? Are you still plagued by that evil woman, the Irish godmother? Did you ever find your childhood love, your Arturo?"

Her eyes widened. "Why, fancy you remembering that!"

"You evade my question. Did you?"

Bianca laughed, and placed a hand on Valentino's knee. "Now, Rudy, that is another story."

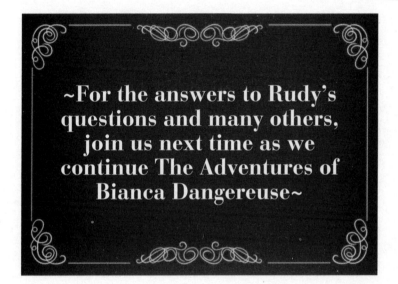

~For the answers to Rudy's questions and many others, join us next time as we continue The Adventures of Bianca Dangereuse~

~Real Or Not Real?~

REAL

Rudolph Valentino—Born in Castellaneta, Italy, in 1895, son of an Italian father and French mother, Valentino came to the U.S. in 1914 and by 1921 was a major motion picture star, the first great romantic screen idol. Well-educated, Valentino spoke five languages, was extremely athletic, and by all accounts, hated being typecast as a Lothario irresistible to women. Toward the end of his life, he often expressed his extreme unhappiness. His personality was much like I represented it here, boyish and naive. He studied agriculture in Italy, and his first ambition was to be a farmer. He died August 23, 1926, at the age of 31, of a perforated ulcer and peritonitis. His last words are reported to be, "Don't worry, chief, I will be all right."

The Son of the Sheik—Valentino did not want to star in the sequel to his earlier blockbuster, *The Sheik* (1921), but his finances were in such disarray in 1926 that he felt he had no choice.

A decorative vase actually did fall on Valentino as he left the stage at the Los Angeles premiere of *The Son of the* Sheik He was knocked unconscious and fell into the orchestra pit but recovered in a few minutes.

Valentino was an expert rider and loved spirited horses. He developed such a fondness for the Arab that threw him twice while he was shooting *The Son of the Sheik* that he bought it.

The night before he fell ill in New York, Valentino went to a small party at Barclay Warburton Jr.'s apartment. Warburton himself was hospitalized with a mysterious ailment shortly thereafter.

After Valentino declared his intent to become an American citizen, Benito Mussolini, the Fascist leader of Italy, banned Valentino's movies from Italian theaters. The wreath of flowers with the inscription "From Benito Mussolini" and the Fascist League of North America honor guard appeared at Campbell's Funeral Home as Valentino's body was being displayed. It was later determined that these were publicity stunts staged by Frank Campbell and George Ullman.

No autopsy was performed on Valentino's body, and the coroner reported that he could not definitely determine the cause of death, two things which contributed to the long-term belief by many conspiracy theorists that Rudy had been murdered. His body was removed from the hospital in a wicker coffin covered by a cloth.

Valentino's body was transported back to California for burial, where he was interred in the family crypt belonging to his friend, influential scriptwriter June Mathis, who passed away in July 1927 at the age of forty and is interred in the same crypt.

George Ullman—Valentino's longtime manager, agent, and closest friend was appointed executor of the star's estate, which was in terrible shape due to Rudy's profligate spending. On December 10th and 11th, 1926, Ullman opened up Valentino's estate, Falcon Lair, and auctioned off most of Valentino's property in order to raise funds to pay the star's outstanding debts. Rudy's brother, Alberto Valentino, accused Ullman of mismanagement, and together with his sister, Maria, sued to have Ullman removed as executor, which he was. After Valentino's death, Ullman authored a book called *Valentino As I Knew Him*. Ullman died in 1975.

Jean Acker—The tale of Jean Acker's ill-fated marriage to Valentino occurred as written. She locked him out of the suite on their wedding night and subsequently refused to live with him. Three years later, while his divorce to Jean was pending, he married costume designer Natacha Rambova in Mexico. As soon as they returned to the States, Jean had Valentino arrested for bigamy. In a particularly Hollywood twist, after Natacha left Valentino in 1925, he and Jean became good friends and were often seen out together. She visited him in the hospital as he lay dying.

Natacha Rambova—Born into a wealthy New Jersey family as Winifred Shaughnessy Hudnut, she was a talented and influential costume and set designer who met Valentino in 1921 while they were both working on the movie *Camille*. Married in 1923, Rudy and Natacha were both artistic and bohemian in their tastes, interested in spiritualism and poetry. Natacha was extremely forceful and managed Valentino's career for a while, even negotiating his contracts, which made her very unpopular among the studio moguls in Hollywood. Fiercely independent, she decided she didn't need the grief and left Rudy in 1925. Later in life she became a noted Egyptologist.

Mary Pickford—Throughout the 1910s and 1920s, Mary Pickford, "America's Sweetheart," was the most popular actress in the world. She was an astute businesswoman, who oversaw every aspect of her films, including casting, scriptwriting, editing, distribution, and promotion. In 1919, she teamed with Douglas Fairbanks, Charlie Chaplin, and D. W. Griffith to found United Artists Studios, which was created to give actors more control over their own projects.

Douglas Fairbanks—A top box office draw, he starred in blockbuster silent movies like *The Three Musketeers, The Thief of Baghdad,* and *Robin Hood.* The affable and athletic Fairbanks married Mary Pickford in 1920, and together, they became Hollywood's first power couple. In 1927, Fairbanks was elected the first president of the Motion Picture Academy of Arts and Sciences and was the first Academy Award presenter. That same year, he and Pickford were the first people to have their hands and feet set in cement at Grauman's Chinese Theatre in Hollywood. He and Pickford divorced in 1936. Fairbanks Sr.'s movie career faltered after sound came in, but his son, Douglas Fairbanks Jr., had a successful and long career that spanned the late 1920s all the way to 1981.

Pola Negri—Polish actress Pola Negri's hysterics at Valentino's funeral caused such a furor that her American movie career was effectively ruined. It was widely believed at the time that her grief was faked. The fact that she married a Russian prince less than nine months after Valentino's death didn't help matters. She returned to Europe, where she continued her successful screen career. Negri really was a talented actress, and she maintained until the day she died that Valentino was the great love of her life.

James Quirk—Columnist and editor in chief at *Photoplay* magazine, Quirk was indeed a good friend of Valentino's who interviewed him, reviewed his movies, and wrote opinion pieces about him. He was present in New York when Valentino died and was a pallbearer at Valentino's New York funeral. Quirk died in August 1932. Several years later, his nephew, Lawrence Quirk, wrote that his uncle had told him that before the funeral, George Ullman arranged to have Valentino's body replaced by a wax image.

Rex Ingram—The noted Irish-born producer and director directed Valentino in his first major film, *The Four Horsemen of the Apocalypse*. He never directed a movie called *Grand Obsession*, since that film is only a figment of my imagination, but it is true that Ingram and Valentino did not get along.

George Fitzmaurice—The director of Valentino's last film, *The Son of the Sheik*, Fitzmaurice was a prolific director who helmed over eighty movies for several different studios from 1915 until shortly before his death in 1940.

Barclay Warburton Jr.—Known to his friends as "Buzzy," Valentino's friend Warburton was the grandson of department store founder John Wanamaker and was a fixture in Philadelphia society.

Bela Lugosi—The Hungarian actor, most famous for starring in the 1931 movie *Dracula*, was working on Broadway in 1926 (as Count Dracula!) and did not go to Hollywood until 1928, but I thought he would be well cast as the Clutching Claw, so I brought him to Hollywood to play the villain in Bianca's movie a bit earlier than the date he actually arrived.

Fakir Rahmin Bey—The popular illusionist from Egypt appeared at various venues around New York City in 1926. Valentino did see his show and was pierced through the arm by a long needle as part of the act, but this occurred at the 300 Club (owned by

Texas Guinan, who was quite a colorful character herself) while he was in town promoting *The Son of the Sheik*, and not at Barclay Warburton's apartment.

Campbell's Funeral Church—Founded in 1898 by Frank Campbell, the funeral home now known as Campbell's Funeral Chapel is still going strong. The earthly remains of anyone who is anyone who dies in New York City will probably be lovingly disposed of by Campbell's. Some of the famous names whose funerals were handled by Campbell's include Jacqueline Kennedy Onassis, Joan Crawford, John Lennon, Greta Garbo, and the Notorious B.I.G. The funeral of Valentino, which was the biggest ever seen by the city up to that point, was an even more outrageous circus than depicted in this novel.

Anthony Cornero (Tony the Hat)—Cornero was a notorious bootlegger with a fleet of ships that he used to haul whiskey from Canada, but in the fall of 1926, when this novel takes place, he had not yet gotten into the gambling ship business. In December 1926, he was arrested at the Mexican border while trying to enter the U.S. with a load of rum and sentenced to two years in prison. While being transported to jail, Cornero escaped the guards and jumped off the train, finally making it to Europe, where he spent a few years in hiding. Eventually, he did return voluntarily to the U.S. to serve out his sentence. Upon his release, he took up where he left off and opened a series of very popular gambling ships for "ordinary people" up and down the California coast. He often bragged that no one was ever cheated in one of his floating casinos.

Gambling ships—I was premature in my depiction of floating casinos. The first experimental gambling ship appeared off the California coast in the summer of 1927 and was shut down immediately by the Los Angeles district attorney. However, the idea had been planted, and by the early 1930s, several gambling ships were anchored off the coast just outside U.S. jurisdiction. U.S. Marshals did occasionally use a 1793 law about "pirate craft" to seize vessels when they had the opportunity. The idea of the imaginary *Monaco* burning was inspired by the following article from the *Dallas Morning News*, September 1, 1930:

> LONG BEACH, Cal., Aug. 31 (UP)—Deep sea divers Sunday worked for hours under the sea in a vain effort to locate a vault containing $50,000 in silver, currency and checks lost late Saturday night when the gambling ship *Monfalcone* sank after a spectacular fire. The notorious craft was set afire by a leaking gasoline line and a spark from a motor. It burned to the water-line after 300 fashionably dressed visitors were rescued by water taxies and other small boats which put out from Seal Beach, six miles from where the *Monfalcone* lay at anchor. Thomas Jacobs, proprietor of the boat, said he estimated his loss at $110,000 in gambling and kitchen equipment and machinery. Jacobs paid a tribute to musicians who played lively music until all the passengers had been removed. Three employees of the boat suffered minor burns attempting to extinguish the flames.

H. L. Mencken—A mere week or so before his death, Valentino had lunch with the noted journalist and critic, whose work he admired, to seek advice on how to handle the virulently nasty press he had been the brunt of for years. Mencken advised him to ignore it. Valentino chose to challenge his latest detractor, a columnist with the *Chicago Tribune* who had called him "a pink powder puff," to a boxing match. When the challenge was declined, sportswriter Frank "Buck" O'Neil volunteered to step in. The match took place on the roof of the Ambassador Hotel in New York. Valentino knocked out O'Neil with one punch. After Valentino died, Mencken wrote a touching memorial to him in the August 30, 1926 edition of the *Baltimore Evening Sun*. Mencken included the essay in his collection, *A Mencken Chrestomathy: His Own Selection of His Choicest Writing*. The entire essay can also be found online. My favorite quote by Mencken on Valentino is: "He was precisely as happy as a small boy being kissed by two hundred fat aunts."

MAYBE REAL, MAYBE NOT

Jenny—Jenny Donahue is a figment of my imagination. However, George Ullman reported that Valentino called out several times for a "Jenny" when he was in the ambulance on his way to the hospital. Ullman speculated that "Jenny" was one of the spirit guides with whom Valentino communed regularly. Valentino was a firm believer in life after death and spirit guides and made no secret of it. His major spirit guide was a Native American called Black Feather.

NOT REAL

Bianca LaBelle, née Blanche Tucker

Fee, surname (or perhaps first name) unknown.

K. D. Dix, gangster queen

Ted Oliver, private detective

Miles Donahue, oil magnate

Marty Levinson, publicity director for United Artists

Caroline White, wardrobe mistress for United Artists

Orange Garden, Bianca's estate in Beverly Hills

Alma Bolding, actress, Bianca's mentor

Nils Fox, director of the Bianca Dangereuse movies

Daniel May, Bianca's co-star

Baldy, tough guy

"Juan," even tougher

Raffaello Guillermo, farmer

Grand Obsession, Bianca's movie with Rudolph Valentino

The Clutching Claw, the eighth film in the fictional *Adventures of Bianca Dangereuse* series

About the Author

By Donald Koozer

Donis Casey is the author of *The Wrong Girl*, Book #1 of the Bianca Dangereuse Hollywood mysteries, set in the 1920s and nominated for the 2020 Oklahoma Book Award.

Her award-winning Alafair Tucker Mysteries—*The Old Buzzard Had It Coming, Hornswoggled, The Drop Edge of Yonder, The Sky Took Him, Crying Blood, The Wrong Hill to Die On, Hell with the Lid Blown Off, All Men Fear Me, The Return of the Raven Mocker,* and *Forty Dead Men*—feature the sleuthing mother of ten children in Oklahoma during the booming 1910s. Donis has twice won the Arizona Book Award for her series and been a finalist for the Willa Award and a ten-time finalist for the Oklahoma Book Award. Her first novel, *The Old Buzzard Had It Coming*, was named an Oklahoma Centennial Book in 2008. Donis is a former teacher, academic librarian, and entrepreneur. She lives in Tempe, Arizona.